Hyperreality

"There is a constant sense that my life is listening to something else. Something adjacent. On my left side, there is something solid. What's solid is dark inside; what's dark is infinite. Only a surface accepts light—or what is light accepts only a surface. The eye is half-light, half-surface: a glass for reading something un-intelligible. For a poet, God is something to be sought and stumbled upon, a statue sleeping under weeds. What is God to a novelist? God is nothing, nowhere. God is one pellet in a hailstorm, a weed to be uprooted. There is no Absolute Other, only a magnetic and soporific otherness. We sense this otherness and sometimes call it reality, but in all this looking, sniffing, hexing, biting, and clawing, it never appears. I don't think it's going to rear up and bare its face. If it ever does, I don't know I'll see it… because I still don't know what I am. I could be a microorganism in the stomach of a great turtle. One night, on the phone with an ex-lover, I called myself a *fucking worm*. I dreamed that I was sawed in half; nothing changed. A part of me is unphased, unmoving, does not want to remember, does not forgive, does not see. I am waiting for a mirror to reflect a little light from somewhere in the hills. Not a light of warmth but a light of cool water. I need a flood to rinse away the mucus that came in with the world. I see a baby deer, naked, curled in a cavity, pressing its head to the wall, sending these words, shaking, barely thinking. I have no hope, no money, no magic tricks. And I don't know the meaning of the word transformation. I guess that's what humans have done to the Earth, but when I speak of Earth, though I see the Ohio River, I still don't know what I'm saying. I've heard we were less than dust and became dancing snakes, then squirrels, then apes, then bare trees; then were crucified, thrown into a cave and trapped, reawakened, and made a little fire. This was the first fire—and the first mirror. There are no windows. The eye, too, is a mirror."

I finished reading this opening paragraph, dropped my printout, and looked at the workshop circle. The classroom's walls were gold-white, halved by a dark blue line. The light was bright and twinkling.

Ralph, the instructor, said, "Thank you, Luis. Someone, tell us what his piece is about."

Iris raised her hand. "The story has two sections," she said. "The first is told in an experimental, stream-of-consciousness style by an unnamed narrator. The second is told by the first narrator's twin brother, Apollo, who is gay, and is a student here at WVU, and whose boyfriend cheats on him with their math professor. The first brother thinks in images and poetry, and Apollo thinks in logic and reason."

"I thought that the first brother was in a coma and had amnesia," Danielle said. "That would explain why everyone he mentions is named for a Greek god or goddess—because he doesn't remember the real names."

A few people grunted and nodded. Ralph raised his eyebrows. His eyes moved to the bottom of the first page, and he read: "'There are no windows. The eye, too, is a mirror.' What does that mean?"

"I've been thinking about that," Isaiah said, gazing at the ceiling. Isaiah was an environmental science major who did dabs every day. "Because the word 'mirror' seems important to the piece. I circled every time it comes up, and it does—" He flipped to the last page, where he'd jotted it down. "—twenty-two times."

"Well," Truth said, "he has an identical twin, so they're like mirrors of each other."

"Yeah," Kristen said, "and Apollo is gay, so..." She seemed to lose confidence. "That's a kind of mirroring, too? I don't know."

Ralph grinned and leaned back in his chair. He seemed to gaze past the circle, beyond the room. "Ah, yes," he said, "it does happen that we mirror our partners in relationships. In James Baldwin's great *Giovanni's Room*, the protagonist, David, often considers how the fate of his lover, Giovanni, is interchangeable with his own. At the end of the novel, as Giovanni is waiting to be executed, David looks in a mirror and reflects that he, too, is *under sentence of death*—as are we all."

"I thought the brother was a figment of his imagination," Truth mumbled.

There was a pause. Ralph said, "Kristen. Tell us what you liked about the piece."

"Um, I don't know," Kristen said, bristling. She was a nursing major who had clearly never read anything above Nicholas Sparks or *The Hunger Games*, but was the only person in these workshops who consistently brought in pieces that dealt with actual human, i.e., sexual, relationships, and was therefore my favorite classmate. She continued: "Clearly, the author is smart and has an amazing vocabulary. But honestly, a lot of this story went over my head, no matter how much I highlighted. I didn't know what was going on."

"I had the same thing," Truth said. "I wanted more dialogue—especially for the first part. I know it was supposed to be stream-of-consciousness. I just found it very abstract."

Ralph rubbed his chin. "There's a vignette—I think it's on page five." He found it and read: "'I close my eyes in eons of crumbling dirt and roaring sound. I open my eyes and see Selene beneath a neon sign, laughing, baring her teeth, standing with six other girls.'" He raised his eyes. "What does this suggest about the narrator?"

"You can kind of tell that he likes this girl," Kristen said.

"Would we call them *girls*, or would we call them *young women*?"

Ralph turned to me as he asked this, so I answered, "Girls."

"What if they were male?" Ralph pressed. "Then would you call them boys?"

Before I could answer "yes," the classroom door was flung open. A wave of terror passed through me; it was easy to imagine that whoever entered could be holding an assault rifle.

But it was just Damon, out of breath, moving in his typical brutish, lumbering way. He went around the circle and took the empty desk on my left. As Truth argued that the story needed "more sense of smell," Damon unzipped his backpack and took out a cheap, battered notebook and a mangled copy of my piece. In the corner of my eye, I saw him hurriedly writing a feedback letter.

Ralph summed up the critique by saying he liked my "rhapsodizing" but that I should find ways to root it more in scene and dialogue. He added that

I should include "more sense of smell." He asked if I had any comments.

I said, "Heraclitus wrote that if all things were smoke, we would navigate the world by smell. Because society relies primarily on language, we depend on our eyes and ears. For me, memories are visual and auditory. Smell is strongly connected with memory, but I don't remember a smell by itself. A sudden confrontation with a smell recalls past images and atmospheres. It's never concisely the smell of mowed grass, espresso, incense; I remember the smell of a situation, a person, a room. These smells don't have names. It could be that smell and memory are the same thing."

"Damon," Ralph said. "Glad you made it. Will you read us the first page of your piece?"

"Uh," Damon said, glancing into his backpack. "I actually don't have a copy. Can I borrow—" I handed him my printout, which was almost fifty pages and seemed unedited.

I looked around the room. People were bouncing their legs, wringing their hands. Iris scratched her neck. I felt my gut roiling.

When Damon finished reading, Ralph asked, "Can someone tell us what the story is about?"

Danielle volunteered: "It's about a *young man* who drops acid and has a bad trip where his cat talks to him, and he sees a strange orange fluid floating in his kitchen. The next day, he gets up and walks to work. He gets there late because he stops to help a homeless man pay for the bus. His boss is an African American dwarf—can I say dwarf?—who orders him to write an article bashing Donald Trump, which he doesn't want to do because he doesn't care about politics. After work, he goes to a coffee shop and interacts nervously with a girl who works there. She pressures him to ask her out, so he does. At dinner, they talk about beer, music, football, kissing, and sex. Then they go back to her apartment and have sex."

"Great," Ralph said, glancing around. "Kristen. What did you like about the piece?"

Kristen answered, "Honestly—nothing." Her voice was trembling. "I thought this guy was an entitled asshole with a toxic attitude towards women."

It felt good, sort of, to hear this vindication of what most people in the room were surely thinking. At the same time, the roiling in my gut kept intensifying. As more voices added to the discussion, the same issues were reiterated with growing fervor. Beside me, Damon's leg was bouncing so aggressively that my desk vibrated; the water in my Nalgene rippled continuously.

The critique ended; Ralph asked Damon to comment. In the unhinged vibrato of someone in a state of high anxiety, Damon said, "I'll say, first thing, that I have no respect for anyone. Everything I think about another human being is either a categorical condemnation, debasement, degradation, or admonition of some kind—either that or a fragile, meager caveat to provisionally convince myself against the proposition that all people are sad, disgusting monsters. Also, something about men is that no one loves them or wants them. And while this makes them more free, it also means their sense of *subjectivity* is impaired. The gap between what a man says and doesn't say is very narrow. Maybe I'm just talking about myself. But I just wanted to share something real."

He went on to say something about political correctness, something about cancel culture, something about *A Room of One's Own*. Everyone stared at their desk or the floor, withdrawn.

♦

It was 6:30PM, Friday, December 6, 2019. The hallway of the main level of Woodburn Hall was quiet, empty, twinkling with the gold light of chandeliers reflecting in the white tile. I knelt beside the door of the classroom to tie my shoelace and tidy the contents of my Janus Films tote bag—my water bottle, the stack of annotated copies of my piece, a separate stack of feedback letters on ruled paper, a Christmas card from my uncle Clayton, a notebook, a red gel pen, a blue ballpoint pen, a worn Penguin Classics copy of *Madame Bovary*—then stood and went to the big brass doors at the back end of the atrium, the inside of the building's brooding front whose clock tower looms above the staggering drop of Woodburn Hill. The right-side door swung open on bluing limestone steps.

Snow was falling. There was the courtyard, lamplit, with bricks encircling a wintered shrub, that some of my peers called the Acropolis—for the view pours out and over the night of vast, vaporous, streetlight-smeared, tree-blurred shadow; of smears of dull tin, branches and shingles swiping, etching themselves in the coarse backs of the hills as they tumble to the Monongahela River. As I descended I looked up through the light to the sky: snowflakes, illuminated, fell in white and gray screens; space was a silent wall of steel, faintly scratched; the clouds were oblong rays of silver, anonymous, smooth and somber; only where the power plant's spire chimney—a long black needle striking straight up—cast its red flare against the fog: an uproaring, rumbling passage of smoke was revealed. It disappeared as I passed the silhouette of a tree.

I moved around the corner of the building and saw Danielle walking up ahead. She wore a long, gray wool coat, a red cashmere scarf, and a leather backpack. Danielle was a self-identified "recovering Catholic," and though she had attempted to expurgate her Catholicism through partying and other sins, she retained the deep simultaneous ecstasy and shame that make Catholicism the last fortress of eroticism. We had slept together once, out of the blue, after she texted me late one night and asked me to come over. Afterward, we remained friends, but she kept her distance. I could only theorize the cause—and I often did. I jogged to catch up with her. She was smoking.

"Rough day," I said, gesturing for a cigarette. We stopped walking. She gave me one and lit for me.

"That guy is such a dog," she said. "Are you going to the thing tonight?"

"Probably," I said. "Are you?"

"Probably not. I promised my roommate we'd get stoned and watch *Blue Planet*." As she said *Blue Planet*, her phone buzzed in her hand. She checked it. Her eyes widened; her hand went over her mouth.

"You know the kid who got shot at College Park the other night? He just died."

I checked my own phone. I had the same email, plus a text from Hannah that read: "Are you coming to 123 tonight? I'll be there and I have ketamine to share."

I cleared my notifications and looked up at Danielle. "That's sad," I said.

♦

The radiator in my dorm room was broken. When I'd moved in it hadn't worked at all, so when it got cold I filed a maintenance request; then one day I came into the room and it was scorching, dry and unbreathable. Now, even in the winter, I kept a box fan in the window to offset the heat.

Tonight, as usual, I came in, dropped my tote by the door and stripped to my underwear. I glanced at the Girl with the Pearl Earring postcard beside the light switch, dropped down and plugged in the string lights. In the kitchenette I opened the particle board cupboard and took out the last packet of peanut butter crackers. As I ate the crackers, leaning back on the tiny counter, I texted Hannah: "Yes, I'll be there."

A moment later, she texted back, "Are you reading?" I said no.

When the crackers were gone I went around the bar counter, collided with the bed and lay grinding my nose into the pillow. Feeling a stir in my groin, I plucked a tissue from the box beside the bed, opened Pornhub, and masturbated to a video titled "POV Beautiful Teen Elf Girl Suck Dildo Deepthroat Dick and Doggy Style with Cumshot." Afterward, I dropped the tissue on the wood floor and turned to face the wall. The heat and the whirring of the box fan seemed to coalesce in the glowing dark. Feeling that warm oscillation as a vaguely brilliant cycle of thought, I fell half asleep. When I woke I looked up at the water-stained hole in the ceiling and then at the far wall, at a black and white photo of Pasolini.

I'd slept about forty minutes; the open mic had started. I got up and put on new underwear, new socks, black jeans, a purple collared shirt, a two-tone black and teal puffer coat, a black scarf, Doc Martens. I pocketed my phone and wallet, went into the bathroom, pissed, washed my hands, and went out.

In the stairwell I plugged in AirPods and put on "Isn't It a Pity" by Nina Simone. Sad piano stirred in my ears; I went out to the courtyard where tall lampposts lit dead ginkgo trees trembling with vibrations from unseen machinery. The gravel beds and concrete shone from the freezing rain. The street was in ambiance, gleaming, humming with chaotic potential; the cars cascading down the brick street were melancholy, severely inclined, capable of murder. Frozen droplets bit my face as I surveyed the frat and sorority houses, their Greek letters darkly glowing, superimposed on the night sky. It was a typical Friday night, still in its early stages: High Street was not yet thronged with clubgoers; a few lost souls could be seen drifting about: sorority girls in tight red and black dresses, some of them shadowed by tall boyfriends scrolling Instagram while walking, dodging uncertain swaths of garbage. On a church staircase sat silent bums, faces masked in quivering darkness, water dripping from their gray hoods. Everything was wet, even the warmly lighted interiors of bars; everything was translucent. I walked slowly, still with Nina Simone in my ears; her voice carried me to the venue. As I came to the door, a hunched homeless guy ran past me; he was holding his back and screaming. I turned, stepped through the doorway, paid the $5 cover, got a neon orange wristband, and proceeded into the cavernous room.

It was an open mic. Onstage, a neatly dressed young woman was belting an Imagine Dragons song and strumming a ukulele. Near the edge of the crowd I spotted my twin sister, Bella, and her boyfriend, Zac. I approached them and asked if they'd seen Hannah.

"Who?" Zac said.

"Hannah," I repeated, enunciating more. They both shook their heads. I turned and went through a doorway to the upper bar, where black steel silhouettes of Kokopelli were floating, backlit with amber light, by the ceiling. I halted in an empty space by a closed circle of people, then someone called my name. It was Otto, president of the philosophy club, my most "alpha" friend, sitting in a round booth with a big group. As I approached, I identified Ben and Gianna, his roommates; Edward, who I vaguely understood as his coke dealer; and three girls I didn't know.

"Come here, you crazy, beautiful man," Otto yelled over the noise. I took a seat next to Autumn, a brunette with icy blue eyes, perfect teeth, and freckles. I asked if anyone had seen Hannah. Those who knew Hannah all muttered, "No."

"Are you reading tonight?" Gianna asked. She was yelling, but I could barely hear her over the noise.

"No," I said. "I don't have any new poems."

Otto grinned at Autumn et al. "This beautiful male specimen is a true poet," he yelled, indicating me. "Maybe the greatest living poet."

Then he looked at me. "So what, bro? Read some old shit, read anything. I don't even know who's reading tonight, but they probably suck." Gianna was silent, but her face expressed tacit agreement. Then she brightened. "Read something for us," she said. "Autumn is visiting from Baltimore. Autumn, Luis really is a good poet."

I smiled, dropping my face. "There is this poem that's been stuck in my head," I said. It was also the only poem I knew by heart. "It's called 'The Sick Rose.' It's by William Blake." I closed my eyes and recited:

> *"O Rose, thou art sick.*
> *The invisible worm,*
> *That flies by night*
> *In the howling storm:*
>
> *Has found out thy bed*
> *Of crimson joy:*
> *And his dark, secret love*

Does thy life destroy."

I opened my eyes. Everyone was quiet. Otto was grinning. "Man," he said. "Some nights, I get so lonely and horny that I writhe in bed and wish I could tunnel into my mattress, and it makes me wonder if I was a worm in a past life."

◆

Gradually I zoned out. I was looking at a crimson chandelier that was hanging in a sphere of pure dark a few meters from the bar, then my eyes scanned down to find Amari standing directly beneath it. The red anti-glow made her black skin appear ultraviolet, holographic. She was looking at her phone but spotted me as I walked over.

We exchanged hellos and half-hugged. I asked if Hannah was around.

"She's not," she said. Her voice seemed full of empathy. "She was supposed to be."

I nodded at the tarnished floor. In the corner of my eye, Amari's phone screen flashed on; she checked Instagram. I thought for a second, then looked up.

"Hey," I said, "do you have—"

"Come on," she said, beaming. As she led me across the bar, I watched her dark blue sweater shifting on her shoulders. She led me down the back hallway, past a few figures unpacking instruments from hard cases, up to the twin doors of the restrooms. Amari knocked on the ladies' door, put her ear to it, then cracked it open. No one was looking. We stepped inside.

It was dark—the light switched on—the light was an epithelial screen fixed above the grimy mirror. The walls were wine red, bright with translucent graffiti runes in black, green, yellow, and silver. The wide-throated toilet was missing its lid; the seat was flecked with something like spackle. The tank hood had "RIP LIL PEEP" scrawled in the upper left corner.

I watched Amari's face in the mirror as she stood fixing her eyeliner. When she had finished, she sent two fingers into her jeans' coin slot, pinched and brought out a tiny zip-lock of white powder. She went to the toilet tank, wiped the hood with her wrist, and coaxed out a little pyramid of ketamine. Then she opened her wallet and took out her WVU student ID and a $20 bill. As the card tapped the white ceramic, my phone buzzed against my ribs.

It was a text from Hannah: "Hey, I forgot I was scheduled to work 8-2 tonight. I'm dancing at H2O. You should come hang. There's a cover but I'll get you an Uber."

I texted back, "Bet, sounds fun, yes."

I darked my phone and watched as Amari took her last line. She stepped away and handed me the rolled 20. I rolled it a bit tighter, swooped to the ceramic, and snorted deeply. I took three lines and came back up. Amari was playing with her hair; she turned to me.

"What brand is your sweater?" I asked. "I like it a lot."

"Thanks!" She ran her right forefinger down her left arm. "It's thrifted, so, I don't know."

◆

As I turned the doorknob to leave, I felt something like a dark glistening wallpaper shedding itself from the walls of my mind. The hallway and the figures hanging around it were electric, dark pink and luminous. There were drums going hard, steady and loud, electric guitar shrieking like a razor, the crowd around the bar morphing together as one mammoth creature. My eyes flickered shut as I passed through this enormous body, a mass so dark and rambling that my inner eyelids were lighter, like gray slate, and on the slate there was a shaded Picassoid sketch of a buffalo with daggering shoulders and hundreds of legs, the detail was immaculate, the flower-like hooves were bronze and glittering, it was charcoal. There was an astounding continuity between this image, evolving somehow, and the image I received as I turned into the main room. It seemed I could read the age of the long wood benches by their deep, regular notches, cracks, and scars. The cavernous walls' stickers and scrawlings were faded tattoos, darkly grooving, softly shining from the light of some tall amber lanterns whose flames were reflected in a few small mirrors. The benches were empty; everyone was packed close to the stage. The black metal band was seven stoic, burly men with stringy hair and the heavy features of Neanderthals. There were no vocals; the drums formed a wave that carried the guitar as smogging ruins of an ancient city, the synthesizer beams were little flares, the bass an opaque smokescreen; what was behind was rotating filaments; the dark around the fires stern and sculpted, crackling.

My eyes closed, my body spun around—I saw a green tadpole squirming, burrowing in brown sand—behind me, the surging drums and strings went out like a candle; the crowd was silent; from the synthesizer there persisted a low *Om* and soaring chimes; my eyes opened.

The front of the room was all dark; the door was a mouth through which the silver, pewter, obsidian street appeared as a miracle; it seemed a brilliant, uninvented passage of an immense brutalist latticework, a sculpture the size of a city. Snow fell in the frame with no sense, no time. My body moved out to the light.

Some cars—they had the aura of giant, magical beasts—climbed the road, which was slick and shining. My head darted around to accept the cold night. My lips felt lush and hot. I yearned for a cigarette; the yearning felt good. A flat red car with feline headlights came up the street and pulled up over the curb. A morbidly obese woman stuck her head out from the driver's seat.

"You're Luis?" She called out to me. My body went to the backseat, got in, scooted to the right side.

The car was warm and thick with an aroma of multiple air fresheners: vanilla and cinnamon clips on the vents, two pine trees and a perfumed coyote's foot hanging from the rearview, a mulled cider candle lit and liquid in a cupholder folding out from the dash. In front of me, on the passenger seat headrest, a red pentagram was sewn into the gray fabric. "For protection," the driver explained. The cabin lights went out and we fell silent. When the car started moving I felt it was merely articulating the kind of motion I'd been feeling all night. I sat with closed eyes viewing multicolored, pixelating tubes entwining in a void.

I put in my AirPods and scrolled through Twitter, clicking on the first video that came up: Melania and Donald Trump officiating the lighting of the National Christmas Tree. The First Lady wore a red and white plaid coat—candy cane colors. It was night; there were garlands and green wreaths with red ribbons, white lights twinkling all around, a piano playing "Hark! The Herald

Angels Sing" adagio. Trump kissed his wife on the cheek and went to the podium.

"All across our land, Melania and I would like to wish you a very, very Merry Christmas," he said. "And now the First Lady will do the honors of lighting the National Christmas Tree. So, we'll count down from five to that very special number..."

The car pulled into a parking lot and stopped. I mumbled thanks to the driver and stepped out onto gravel lit by a single towering streetlamp. I took in the facade of the club, a corrugated warehouse-like building with a vinyl banner tethered above the door: "H2O: Bar & Exotics." The front door was a slab of dull, dusty steel. I pulled it open.

There was a short, dark corridor met promptly with a booth where a bouncer was stationed. He asked for my ID, then asked for the cover. It was $20. I used my phone to check my bank account—I had about $120. I went to an ATM in an alcove near the booth and took out $40. The bouncer took my coat and lobbed it into a closet.

The club's walls were mirrored, graphed with pink neon; the floors were black marble. "Hell of a Life" by Kanye West blared from a speaker system. The dancers were hanging out at the bar and on black leather couches. Some were coupled with sweating, grinning men with bad teeth and hair; four were clustered together, whispering and laughing. One of these four was Hannah. Eventually, she noticed me and came over, moving awkwardly in platform heels. She put her hands on my shoulders, kissed my cheeks and said, "I'm still learning to walk in these things."

We went to the bar. I started a tab, and we took shots of Hennessy. I asked Hannah if she liked her job.

"Sure," she said. "I just get wasted every night. The girls are mostly great. And at the end of the night we all get driven home—to make sure nothing happens. Which is nice."

I nodded. I was watching a young woman with cropped, dyed black hair, a long neck, prominent shoulder blades. She was conversing with a tall country boy in steel-toe boots, a tacky flannel, and a camouflage hat with a fishhook on the bill. I could see she was a little drunk: she kept shifting her posture, couldn't stand still; her head swayed when she laughed. Behind her, on one of the couches, an older black man, bald, with striking features, well dressed, wearing a jeweled bolo tie and rings, was staring at her with sharp, steady eyes. Tracking my gaze, Hannah said, "A lot of the job is dealing with guys like that. He'll do anything to get one of us to leave with him, but no one will. We never do."

She led me to the back of the room, to the stage. A muscular woman with a yellow-blond pixie cut and orbicular breast implants was high on the pole, upside down, her toned shoulders angled toward the Earth. She was spinning; her eyes were closed.

"That's Luna," Hannah said. "We're not supposed to watch each other dance. I'll be at the bar."

I took a seat in one of the shabby lounge chairs that made a ring around the stage. On my left sat a middle-aged man with a beer gut stuffed under a white collared shirt and khakis. His round nose and cheeks were dotted with pimples. His eyes watered; his mouth hung slightly open, pursed and smiling, trembling slightly, like a baby craving breastmilk, teetering forward in un-hinged eagerness to gaze up at Luna as a worm gazes up at the moon.

On my right, another man, altogether similar, just a little thinner, was slumped; he seemed bored to shit. He was holding a clear plastic cup of what looked like blue Powerade. As I observed him—he never looked my way; he was still, in some way, transfixed—he fished a wad of ones from his pocket, peeled a few off and pitched them onto the lip of the stage. Luna was still up in space, turning and turning. She was an impressive athlete. When her song ended she gathered her bills and walked back along the catwalk to disappear behind a black curtain.

For a moment there was no music; the speakers and pink neon buzzed. I watched the curtain swaying, swaying, then shocking with air, something moving behind it—*Behold:* the figure who emerged did not immediately settle in my sight; she seemed to enter deeper, deeper in my eyes with every step, every slash of leg. The lights around the stage were the sheerest water pouring up from her shoulders, rinsing her ears. My eyes moving down her body forgot they were eyes, became a tongue; my tongue lifted up in my mouth. Every inch—her towering neck, her collarbones, her breasts, still hidden under bloodred lace, her navel, painfully bear, the crowns of her hips demanding the elegant term *iliac crest*, paroxysmal crests I wished were my first two knuckles, burning rings seeming to mouth the word crest better than the word can be spelled—cut me from within like a crackhead heartbeat of the neck, a whole note in memory, the squealing click of the latch of the bathroom door in my grandparents' house, incomprehensible, scratching the very root of my brain. At her touch, the pole, that gleaming nothing, became flesh, flesh in a mirror, a mirror of my own flesh. I wanted to gnash it apart, to be that thing, that feeble instrument, that cold and dire needle—a sliver of matter utterly inaccessible—her hand was stroking it. Her palms glancing over her breasts, an airplane crashing, very quick, undoing the hooks between the cups of her bra, *behold*—those erect brown nipples. Her hand with its polished nails was the passage of time, creating and erasing. Her fingernails were violet windows to deep space. They fell upon her thighs with such complicated force. Her thighs were two walls; what was between them was a magnet of incalculable torque; the place itself held its breath as her hips rocked; microscopic reaches of the room held breath in fear that one reality could be destroyed by another. The world was but a sigh as she removed her thong; it seemed to burn away, go straight into nothingness, and now there was just a G-string, a black star, a singularity of cloth; it wobbled in the air like the tip of a laser and plunged down, those legs and pretty feet, still in platform heels, massive weights tethering a goddess—erupted toward *me*, furiously turned, her knees kissed the drooling stage, her ass shook in my face, she pinched both poles of the G-string and stretched it—now the thread of the cosmos scanned around her hips, I saw her asshole, her ass cheeks hot, tight, her labia framed in the darkest divine rudiments that taught me anew the word *skin*, that taught my tongue its own name, unspeakable, that thudded in my mouth and my throat and my chest like rocks falling, drumming against the earth, speaking, like napalm.

◆

"That's Cherry," Hannah told me. We were at the bar, taking more shots. Cherry had just reappeared in the room. "I'm pissed at her. Earlier she stole a lap dance from me."

She was coming toward us. When she reached the bar and sat, Hannah touched my shoulder and said, "This is my friend Luis Neer. He's a poet."

Emboldened by alcohol, I tried giving her an open and honest look, but she didn't return it. She looked at the floor, then at Hannah. They made unintelligible banter until Hannah moved away to an older man sitting alone, forlorn.

I sat in a silence void of time, suddenly aware of the materiality of, and continuity between, my body and the room. To move, to talk, even to "think" in some sense seemed impossible. When I finally looked to the left, where Cherry was standing, I was surprised to find her staring, inspecting me. She was maybe 5'5", six inches shorter than me.

I opened my mouth to ask a question, I didn't know what, but something in her look indicated that I should be silent. We looked at each other for a long time. Then she smiled. She asked, "Would you like a private dance?"

◆

We took shots—tequila this time. Then I felt very drunk; my face was on fire with pleasure. She led me by the hand down a hallway that was completely dark. I stared at the back of her head, near the base, where her dark brown hair swayed against her neck. We went to the end of the hall, through a doorway to a room that was dark, too, lit only with a pink neon strip on the back wall. She guided me backward into a chair. She took off my glasses and hung them on my shirt. My head partly blocked the neon behind me, so part of her face was eclipsed from the pink ray; without my glasses, the neon's haze seemed to sway and swirl and flicker on her cheeks. She pinned my hands against the couch and grinded on me. I studied her eyes. In the phosphorescent reflection of her pupils, I almost thought I could see myself—for a moment. Then she turned her head down and to the side very slightly. In her left eye, all the light left. Her right eye flamed in such a way that I momentarily sensed some truth revealing itself. I grasped for what it was; it rippled out in my mind, away from me. She was studying me too. We could hear trap music from the main room distorted through several walls. As it swirled around us, as her fingernails traced my neck, as our sexes swirled with some air and space and darkness in between—my palms scanning her copper thighs, her knees—it seemed to lend language to a conversation passing between us in total obscurity, signaled only by the dancing of shadow and light and the twitching, searching and beaming of our eyes, our mouths, and our breath, which was gentle, sweet from tequila. *Seek and change, seek and change*—how our faces moved and were moved. We might have been hearing a song being sung. It was right here. We were the source of it. When it ended, she whispered in my ear, "I want you to stay with me."

♦

So, I stayed. I burned the last of my money, got head flushed down the shitter of the world drunk and partied with these girls. Most of the men had left, incidentally, so the dancers were free to talk to each other; I saw them hitting Juuls, laughing, heard them exchanging algebraic secrets in dark unspeakable tones. My phone died. At some point, I noticed myself sunk in one of the couches, almost supine, listening to dialogue I wish I could remember. I felt the couch holding me, increasingly still, like a carrier spirit hovering above the ocean at night, holding me in its heart, a light orb, seeing me to the shore...

Then, my consciousness collapsed into focus; the alcohol had melted away. Cherry was in Rick Owens sneakers and an XL Givenchy sweater that went to her knees, motioning for me to come to the door. She was explaining to the driver that we were together.

Then we were in the clean backseat of a car. Cherry had her head on my shoulder. I ran my fingers through her hair.

"Cherry," I whispered.

She pulled away. I felt her looking at me, sharply focused. I met her gaze. I was surprised by the lucidity of the moment.

"That's not my real name," she said. "My real name is Diotima."

"Diotima," I repeated. I didn't know what to make of this revelation. Her brown eyes seemed to request a response, but I had nothing to say, so I took her face in my hands and we kissed. She put her hands on my chest, drew herself close to

me, and moved on top of me. Her perfume was
of sage and red earth.

◆

Her apartment was in the northern part of Mor-
gantown, on a hill overlooking the hospital and
football stadium. It had a high, steep roof, six
blinded windows on its front side, an open
breezeway with wooden stairs. We went up to the
second floor, into #2.

Diotima flipped on a lamp by the door. The light
it cast on the room was pale gold, the walls were
off-white and the floors were bright wood. There
was a red Kashan rug; a floral loveseat; a long
bookcase, half full of books; a standing mirror,
cracked near the bottom, with a gilded frame.

I took off my coat. "Where should I toss this?"

"On the couch," Diotima said. She crossed
through the kitchen, into the hallway, into a door
on the left. She turned on the light; it cast a glow
in the doorway. I went after her and closed the
door—it was a bathroom.

She was leaning over the sink, wiping makeup off her face. I stood behind her in the mirror.

"Why are you named Diotima?" I asked.

"My mom's a philosophy professor," she said. "She wrote her dissertation on Plato's *Symposium*. She met my father in Athens while she was working on it."

"Are your parents Greek?"

"My mom is Chinese, and my dad is Iranian," she said. "They're older. They were both Maoists. My dad emigrated in the 1970s during the Revolution. He bumped around a few random countries before he ran into my mother." She splashed water on her face, dried it with a towel, and turned to me. "They met at the Pantheon."

"Parthenon," I corrected.

"Right," she said, smiling.

I stepped forward and put both hands on her neck and kissed her. She wrapped her arms around me and dropped the towel. I moved forward. She moved back. I pinned her against the door, which clicked shut, and grinded my thigh into her crotch. She bit my lip and sucked while moving her hand under my shirt. She gripped my belt buckle. I bit her neck, grabbed her hips and turned her around, grabbed a fistful of her hair and pressed her face against the door. I undid my belt with one hand; with the other, I reached under the hem of her sweatshirt and fingered her. I felt my wrist knocking against her tailbone. She pulled the sweatshirt off and unhooked her bra while I kissed and bit down her back. I felt her clawing at my thighs. She turned, dropped to her knees, and took me in her mouth. I groaned. I watched her. After a minute or so, I pulled her up and turned her around. She planted her hands on the door and adjusted her stance. As I waited, panting, I happened to glance back at a frosted window on the opposite wall. It was filled with an opaque, featureless gray. When Diotima was set, I tried to push inside her.

"Fuck," I said, stepping back. "I'm sorry. We drank so much tonight."

She wiped some spit from her mouth. "It's okay," she said. She gave a long, strong look—to prove that she was unphased.

◆

We showered together, dried off with the same towel, and went into the bedroom. A large picture of a white tree with red and green flowers on a blue background, framed with white flowering vines flanked by identical rosebushes, was centered on one wall. There were pages of Islamic art from *National Geographic*; postcard-sized prints by Klimt, Matisse, O'Keefe, and others I didn't recognize; a few small mirrors, a white-painted vanity, an old wooden bookshelf topped with a lamp and pencils and notebooks. I stood naked by the door while Diotima dug into a small wood dresser in the closet. She put on a matching set of silk pajamas, baby blue.

She tossed me a pair of sweatpants and a big white T-shirt. As I got dressed, she went to the window and brought up the blinds. "I'm going to make tea," she said.

As she was leaving the room, I asked, "In the *Symposium*, whose speech was your favorite?"

She stopped, turned around, and leaned in the doorway.

"Aristophanes," she said and quoted: "*Human nature was originally one and we were a whole, and the desire and pursuit of the whole is called Love. There was a time when we were one, but now, because of the wickedness of mankind, God has halved us... and there is a danger that we shall be halved again and go about in bas-relief, like the profile figures with only half a nose which are sculptured on monuments, and we shall be like tallies.*"

I went to the window and leaned on the broad windowsill. A haze emanated from the stadium, out of view, and the hospital lights were flaring into the haze. Cars occasionally passed up and down the hillside road. The sky was all clouds, no stars. While observing all this, I suddenly realized I had left my debit card at the club.

Diotima came back, handed me a mug, and sat on the windowsill. "I used honey," she said.

Her left leg hung down from the sill; her bare toes traced the edge of the mattress. She looked at her phone. "It's 4AM," she said.

Then she was quiet, looking out the window. The steep outline of the black hill was thrust over her shoulder. There were red and blue lights, a neighbor's amber porchlight left on, swirling silver clouds. I took in everything: the glint on the glass, the mattress, the softly glowing air, the closet's wood door, some rumbling mess in the dark behind it.

My head fell back on the pillow. On the bookcase that was her nightstand, on the round, flat base of the lamp, there was a folded piece of notebook paper. "What's this?" I asked.

"A poem," she said. "I just wrote it today—before work."

I started to unfold it. She watched me, still sipping her tea.

There was no title. "Can I read?" I asked.

She nodded. "Please."

I read aloud:

> *"The video whispers*
> *behind a curtain*
> *the crackling wall*
> *the black chair seething*

the electric rose
hot blue coals
my eyes in a mirror
double mirrors
the pilgrim spirit
traveling as a sigh
in me, a baby
with my teething ring
in the backseat
going by a river
tumbling in shadow
water as glitter
the faucet
streaked with toothpaste
or water
the crack in the wall
where Love was sweat
on the face of a phone
I can't comprehend
I will never see it again
that scarlet ribbon
binding two fingers
in a hallway of the lungs
or the heart
unremitting, unforlorn
obliquely recalling
a voice whispering
that this, too, is a river."

I looked up. She was still watching me. It seemed too obvious to say, "That was beautiful," so I said nothing. I folded the page and handed it to her. She took it and left the room, her empty cup dangling from one finger.

Soon we were in bed. With my left arm, which was wrapped beneath her, I reached up to her neck and stroked it carefully. My right hand was touching her thigh. Her left hand was clasped around my wrist. Her right was tucked between her legs. I moved my right hand to her left arm. Our heads adjusted. Our legs moved together. We slept.

♦

Then it was light out. I noticed I had a headache. I turned and saw I was alone, then got up and went to the kitchen.

Diotima was sitting on the couch, drinking water, flipping through a big art book. She asked if I wanted to go somewhere for breakfast. I said I was out of money; I'd left my card at the club. She said it was okay, she would pay.

She gave me a spare toothbrush and we brushed our teeth together. Then we got dressed. I sat on the bed, laced up my boots, and watched as she brushed her hair and put in earrings. She turned to me. She asked, "Ready?"

"Yeah," I said, looking at her. "I just have to grab my coat."

We went to the living room. I crossed to the couch as she went outside. Light and cold air swept in from the breezeway, and with it, someone shouting in Arabic. Two voices shouting. I brought my coat up over my shoulders. There was a shot. Two shots. I turned and rushed out— the sun framed in the space between the second and third floors made a field of light like the eye of God, polarizing, obliterating the black iron railing; at first I saw nothing, the breezeway seemed made of fire; then my eyes adjusted and I saw two young men descending the lower staircase; one was tumbling unconsciously, head folding under him; the other was pushing past, rushing down. I turned and saw Diotima. She was lying half-curled on her side, facing the sun, forehead touching the bottom rail. I moved closer and saw a pool of blood, thick and dark and real, spreading out from her stomach, spilling over the edge of the concrete.

Time froze. I cannot tell if I fell over Diotima's body and cradled it, praying aloud that this was a dream, that I would wake up—or if I spun, stumbled backward, and sat in the open doorway, where the police found me. All I know is that I cried and that the cry split into a scream—and all I knew of history, all events were atoms propagating, thrashing, colliding within the scream. It seemed to break away from my mouth and go on amplifying in isolation, widening, revolving, an aperture panicked by a sense of its own incompleteness. All facts submitted to its mind were scornfully rejected; finally all facts were destroyed but two: loneliness, the smell of smoke. Then the scream went on crying, trying to yawn out some old issue, some hollow and tender blueness, and I held that feeling in my chest, unable to do anything with it, not knowing what to do…

When the police came, they asked if I could describe the nature of my relationship with "the victim," Diotima. I looked at them with burning eyes, unable to speak, hating them. Then they were standing above me, faces out of view, and I heard nothing. My head fell against the left side of the door frame. I focused on the metal's cold touch and closed one eye, then the other.

Cecile

It was a situation where Max had given up completely, or as completely as one can, on the notion of his own sexuality—which entailed that he did not worry as much about his clothes or acne scars but just tried to appear unassuming and clean. It also entailed that he stopped looking at people: he lowered his face as he crossed [–] University's downtown campus, avoided eye contact at all times, and tried to unsee the enormous beauty of the crowds surging around him. Our French class was in [–] Hall. Because he was operating to conceal the fact of his existence as completely as possible, he never entered through the main hallway, which had chandeliers and marble floors and was lined with wooden benches and seemed haunted by soft music, actually the soft echo of voices in low conversation, an effect also observed in cathedrals. Instead, he entered through a side door that led straight to the basement, ducked into the classroom quickly, sat in the front row, took out a book, and read until the start of class.

Giving up on sex also meant giving up on social media, which, as far as Max could tell, mainly functioned as a sexual marketplace plain and simple—or this was the impression that followed inevitably from navigating dating apps: that an app like Instagram is merely auxiliary to an app like Tinder, a source of corroboration that you are a real human being, the person who appears in your photos, a person with a life embedded in some kind of social structure, not depressed or a serial killer. Without Tinder, Instagram still provides a form of existential corroboration, and various means of low-pressure flirting; all its mechanisms are predicated on expressing interest. Max aimed to exile himself from the economy of interest, yet he hoped—albeit with a conscious sense of futility—that someone would take an interest in him.

♦

For a time, as the spring semester was starting, Max didn't notice Cecile. She sat behind him in the second row and kept her face lowered, hidden behind dark brown hair. After week three or four we started to do group work, which entailed rotating our desks to face three or four classmates, all of us writing our names on a sheet of notebook paper, mumbling in pained French. Max's French was poor; Cecile's was competent, even elegant, which, along with her name, gave away that she was French—because her name really was Cecile, I'm not making that up.

She was quiet and shy, so it must have piqued Max's curiosity when one day, distractedly glancing around the room, he saw a piece of metal glinting through the cords of her maroon sweater and inferred that she had nipple piercings. Gradually he began to glance at her face—so finally he saw that she was, he thought, "perfectly beautiful."

If one were to adhere to the standard set by 19th-century novelists, it would be possible to go into precious detail describing Cecile's physical appearance—but because the human brain has been severely degraded by processed food, pesticides, EMF radiation, and countless hours of pornography (mostly registered between the ages of eleven and thirteen, in Max's case)—not to mention frequent and high doses of LSD; evidence suggests that acid is non-toxic, yet it seems to introduce a new uncertainty in consciousness, at least—one would then instantly default to the most vulgar and cliché adjectives, i.e., *round, full, deep, smooth, big*—all words that seem to reference the Venus of Willendorf. Much contemporary scholarship argues against the classic view of the Venus of Willendorf as a "fertility symbol," a masturbation idol—not pornographic per se but porno-tactile, a handheld totem whose varied contours and textures mimic those of the female body. Considering how graphic sensibility has overtaken tactile sensibility in a world of visual media, a world "flooded with images"— and considering the Venus of Willendorf as a contoured, textured, tactile object —well, maybe it's an inaccurate theory, but Max had made love to his smartphone in the same way, caressing a sleek surface, a screen displaying pornography. The site of the desiring function seemed to have shifted from touch to sight, body to gaze—yet considering Cecile's eyes, which had dark circles (which suggested, Max came to speculate, that she was either an insomniac or a "ski bunny," that is, a young white woman with a penchant for complimentary rails of cocaine)—her eyes really were big and bright and round, you might even

say bulging, and her lips—simply put, he wanted
to kiss them.

◆

Cecile began to occupy Max's mind, though not
as someone who bore any relation to him, nor as
a romantic prospect; he continued to assume that
they lived in different worlds—she in the world
of beauty and visibility, he in the world of sexless
anonymity—and that the semester would end, he
would finish his foreign language requirement,
and she would pass out of his life without incident.

Because he was not even masturbating at the
time—or masturbating very little, and only with
pornography, which overrode the immoral work
of cultivating fantasies—it can be honestly said
that Max never thought of Cecile's beauty except
in class, sitting across from her; he never made
her the object of any consistent fantasy, let alone
a plan.

At some point, our five-person group exchanged
Snapchat usernames. Max thought nothing of
this; the exchange easily could've happened
without his awareness.

We were assigned a lot of group work, so gradually Max came to interact with Cecile on a regular basis. Most of their interactions were predicated on translating passages of French literature—folk tales at first, then primarily Laclos's *Les Liaisons Dangereuses*.

One day we worked in pairs; Max was paired with Cecile. They were handed a worksheet; Cecile seized it instantly, aligned it beside her notebook and began translating in silence. Max glanced at where she'd written both their names—Max under Cecile—then followed her hand as she wrote. Her handwriting was almost cursive. It put him in a kind of trance; he imagined they were working together by telepathy. He thought maybe they would speak or make eye contact at some point, but they didn't. Fifteen quiet minutes passed.

At the end of class, Cecile stood up and put on her coat. Max glanced at her face; she was turning, kneeling to zip up her boot. Her facial expression was tired, neutral; her head moved slightly forward, the light fell on her face and caught a trace of a hidden emotion: a "trace of disgust," Max thought. This notion pained him as he left the classroom. He was beside Cecile, they separated in the hallway, by the time he passed through the far exit the incident had disappeared from his mind. Then he wondered if Cecile had also spent those fifteen minutes in a telepathic trance.

◆

Max wasn't very interested in learning French; he was 19, an English major, and identified as a fiction writer; that semester, his coursework centered not on French 204 but on English 247, the first class where he had to read and respond to a play by Shakespeare; the play was *King Lear*. He had been assigned *A Midsummer Night's Dream* in freshman year, but had neglected it pretty heavily, reading just enough to comment in class that a certain passage reminded him of Gucci Mane's verse on "Black Beatles"—then there had been a research paper on *Hamlet* in his last year of high school, but then he'd only skimmed the text while watching the film adaptation with Mel Gibson—and that was ancient history, even at this point, sophomore year, it seemed that way. That happens when you take a lot of acid: the past falls away—one is reborn, truly—in any case Max felt that *King Lear* was his first "confrontation" with Shakespeare, and he couldn't help but view it as a confrontation with the sheer incomprehensibility of the universe. The acid had primed him for that—and what else was he reading? mainly Nabokov, *Pale Fire*—which had the effect of putting him to sleep, he would have been embarrassed to admit—and a few novels by Lispector; so he wasn't deriving any sense of coherence from reading, as is sometimes possible: he was only reading incoherent books.

In this way it's easy to sabotage yourself: give yourself over to the incoherence of the world and cease being able to do anything. Max might have felt somewhat aware that this principle of self-sabotage was the sole mechanism driving his behavior—but he couldn't do anything about it.

◆

Max lived in a single-occupancy dorm room in the Towers, the university's cheapest and most populous housing complex; it was a double room, it had two closets, but one set of furniture. Today, like most days, it was clean; Max had vacuumed the night before. Cold air entered the open window. At night the sky was hazy blue; the room was pitch black until Max lit two lamps, one on the desk and one on the bedside table. He walked to the window and looked out on glowing tennis courts, the PRT station, and the steep hill of [–] Campus, where some buildings' horizontal lines shaped the edge of the earth. On the tallest building there was a single red light; smaller white lights were dispersed among all the buildings.

He alternated laying in bed, sitting on the windowsill, and pacing. Around 8PM, he sat at the desk. A 3-4-page essay on *King Lear* was due the next morning at 11; he'd put it off until tonight, thinking last-minute panic would incentivize writing; now, feeling the friction of the approaching deadline—and feeling suddenly aware that he really hadn't spent much time reading, let alone thinking about, the text—his mind was totally blocked.

After anxiously eyeing his Macbook for some time, he closed his essay .rtf, started a new .rtf, and spent two hours typing a stream-of-consciousness journal entry. Just as he felt that he'd succeeded in analyzing the block on his concentration—that the mental conflict was resolved, he could return to the essay—he received a photo message from Cecile.

It was a selfie; it was well lit, her eyes were shining, it was a good angle; it was captioned, "hey, how's it going?" with a smiling emoji.

The dark blue sky was still darkening; the limited light of the lamps took on a gradient intensity verging on intelligence. Max thought it best to "play it safe"; he responded, "hey, it's going well. how are you?" He angled his selfie so his eyes gleamed in the lamplight.

He had read somewhere—in a carousel post on Instagram, he thought—that you can determine whether someone is interested in you by how much face they show in their selfies. Partial face means tentative curiosity; full face signifies unequivocal, definite interest. After a few rounds of full-face selfies, Max sent his phone number and they switched to text.

Cecile, having responded that she felt "so-so," remained ambivalent as the conversation developed; Max mirrored her ambivalence to unlock, finally, a series of deeper intimations. Cecile finally admitted that she was tired, bored, most of all sad.

Max thought their commiseration somewhat obscene; he was vaguely reminded of a scene in *Madame Bovary,* the scene where Emma and Leon are alone for the first time in a hotel room in Rouen, speaking in increasingly intimate, emotional tones; gradually increasing touch, prolonging eye contact; it's obvious, the whole thing, actually it goes without saying, but anyway it must have interested Flaubert that Rouen is phonetically close to *rien,* nothing—because all this paroxysmal formality means nothing, amounts to nothing. "Sadness is banal, boredom is banal," Max thought, and he felt grateful; it is acceptable for two people to discuss their emotions, and such discussion can justifiably lead them to the point of mutual baseness, mutual banality—at which point it made sense for Cecile to invite him over.

Maybe, they agreed, they would stay up late and study—but one thing was clear, they were going to discuss their suffering; it wasn't much of a precedent, as there always has to be some precedent, but it was enough.

Cecile was, she said, "financially secure"; her parents supported her, so money was no issue. She offered to send an Uber to the Towers. Not wanting to seem too eager, Max went down the hall and showered; when he got back he replied "yes."

He glanced away from his phone. The room had taken on a strange mood: the dresser seemed veiled in a gravity of melancholy, it pulled him over, he witlessly took out a pair of black jeans and a maroon sweater. When he inspected the outfit in the mirror he imagined the clothes, too, were animated with a new, preternatural haze of meaning—but the meaning was encrypted, the encryption was a spell of weighted sadness; it bloomed and swirled in his mind and suggested music. To expurgate the mood—or to lean into his stupor—Max put in his AirPods, opened Spotify, navigated to his library, and played Travis Scott: "Maria I'm Drunk (feat. Justin Bieber & Young Thug)." Then he dropped a few things into his backpack and left the room.

In the hallway he hit his dab pen; in the stairwell he hit it two more times. He felt awed by the spaciousness of the main floor; the high ceiling was immersed in a water-like gloom. Cecile typed and sent a message: "the Uber is a white Tesla." And it was there when he passed through the double doors of the main entrance. His focus locked onto the piano part of the Travis Scott beat. He didn't look at or speak to the driver, just plunged into the backseat and burrowed his face in the clean black fabric. The car rumbled into motion.

Partly because he didn't have a reliable drug dealer, Max had a habit of using music to simulate psychedelic perceptions. He had taken psilocybin mushrooms for the first time in October, 5 months earlier; alone in his dorm room, the world vaporized; his consciousness turned to smoke babbling in a vortex, then disappeared. He woke the next morning amazed that he was still alive. It was a painful, alienating experience, but there was something good about it; it was moody and obviously cosmic. "Maria I'm Drunk" recalled its aesthetic; the resonance felt medicinal. This moment, Young Thug's hook ("Call your friends let's get drunk, call your friends let's get drunk") seemed to morph out of the mouth of a vortex; as the car mounted unseen turns Max imagined passively moving through a fractal darkness where voices were strange, powerful light. Justin

Bieber's voice belted into the void; late in his verse, when he sang the word "intertwined," Max felt a wave of trepidation. The cool air of the backseat seemed disturbed. The wave jolted through Max's mind and soothed as the song ended. In the silence before the next song he could hear the car wheels moving over gravel. The car came to a stop; a bright light fell on his face, diminishing his stupor.

He got out, mumbled "Thank you" to the driver, turned, and looked up at Cecile's building. He recognized it as one of the higher-end student housing options, a mid-rise perched on a hill near [–] Campus; he saw it from afar every day. The front of the building was illuminated; small white lights twinkled around the entrance.

In Max's AirPods a piece by Brahms started, it was violins ebbing up and flowing away, woodwinds responding. As Max approached the door, he imagined he was entering a realm of affluence, delicacy and refinement, or was beginning to think something like this—but the door was locked; he jerked the handle with a violent premonition of doom, an echo of his earlier trepidation.

He made eye contact with a front desk attendant, a cute girl with red hair, who buzzed him in. As he approached the desk she watched him with an expression of drowsy confusion. Max explained that he didn't live here, he was visiting a friend. The attendant was visibly struggling to rouse her focus—which Max understood, noting the ambience of the lobby. Finally the attendant said that he could either take the elevator up or wait for his friend to come down and meet him—so Max, who was gazing at a Keurig on a table by the wall, nodded, understanding that the interaction had been pointless. As the attendant had answered his question the Brahms piece had reached a startling crescendo—he realized this happened often, maybe every time he listened to Brahms, the music always changed erratically—so he fumbled to pause it and made a mental note to remove it from his library. He pressed the button for the elevator and texted Cecile to ask her room number. "461," she responded immediately.

The elevator door opened. Max entered and pressed "4." Soft chimes sounded as the elevator lifted past the second floor, then the third. Max focused on the near silence. The door, humming, opened on a stale hallway. Starting toward 461, the hallway seemed surprisingly mazelike (on the outside, the building didn't seem so complicated); it was long, zigzagging, with pallid light and a mood of extreme hollowness; it called to Max's mind the image of an eviscerated torso. Nauseous, Max vaguely imagined reaching Cecile's room would mean escaping from a desperate, disturbed place, somewhere he might be forced to spend eternity. Within ten digits of 461, he texted: "here." He didn't have to knock. The door opened into a dark living room and he sauntered inside.

Appearing as the door closed, washed in soft light from the kitchen, Cecile did something that seemed to Max profoundly sweet and gentle: standing on tiptoe, she put her hands on his shoulders and kissed him on both cheeks. Then she stepped away. For a moment they stood looking at each other. Their eyes curiously and tenderly scanned each other's face.

Max felt a wave of panic: this was the first time, at least since his exit from "the sexual economy" (which now seemed a vague and paranoid notion), that he'd gazed at another human with this depth of intimacy. He was suddenly aware of the

physicality of both their bodies, their faces especially, as both were marked by a nameless, luminous, emergent property, not just a spark of life
but the sign of something beyond a spark, immaterial, a "living history," Max thought; a lightless,
unseen history collapsing suddenly into being.
Cecile wore a white T-shirt and black yoga
shorts. Her expression seemed tentative; Max felt
an impulse to pin her to the door and kiss her, but
he didn't. Cecile smiled nervously, the moment
seemed broken; she bowed her head, closed her
eyes, and walked into the kitchen. Noting
Cecile's bare feet, Max removed his boots.

"Do you want something?" Cecile asked. "I have
water, tea, this wine." She pointed to the wine, a
Malbec; it was in a blue bottle on the counter, un-
opened.

Max nodded. "Wine, thank you." He took a seat
at a high table.

"Good choice," Cecile said, grinning to herself,
still facing the counter. She opened a drawer and
took out a corkscrew. "I'm still learning how to
use this," she said, turning around. She used the
screw to tear the foil from the cork. Max saw that
she had spoken out of modesty; she removed the

cork without difficulty, poured the wine into coffee cups, and bid Max to follow her into the light of the bedroom.

There were four lamps: a standing lamp in the corner, a desk lamp, one on the bedside table, and, on the dresser, an electric lantern. The corner lamp was a cylindrical white shade hovering over a tall black tripod; it cast a soft, wide halo that made the room generally bright, though its brightness was diminished by the smaller lamps, amber orbs. Some white Christmas lights were strung over the bed. On the desk, an essential oil diffuser breathed a light vapor of lavender. The walls were bare, white, freshly painted. Cecile climbed onto the bed, a twin size with an actual wood frame. Her sculpted ass, clad in black spandex, almost a perfect circle, seemed to absorb all the room's light; it locked into Max's sight as an absolute center, a site for the exchange of vast tantric pains and passions fermenting inside him. Then, as Cecile rotated and sat against the wall, he met her eyes, which had naturally large pupils and were flooded with light; his soul fell silent in awe.

Her eyes closed as she sipped her wine, and then she watched as Max folded his limbs and leaned on the wall beside her. Reaching for something to say, feeling that it didn't matter what was said, she asked, "How was your day?"

"My day..." Max thought, glancing at the ceiling. He understood, too, that the content of his response was not precisely important; that said, he really couldn't remember anything from that day. It took a moment of intense focus to conjure faint mental images of classrooms, images troubled by vague associations; when he recalled "French" and other classes he felt vexed, like any words he could put on these subjects would be awkward and vulgar. "It was fine," he settled on saying.

"I had an English class and a French class," he added, hoping that Cecile would respond by naming her class subjects, which actually, not for any particular reason, interested him.

Cecile nodded. "Nice," she said. "I had a biology lab this morning, then statistics, then French."

Max sipped his wine. Then he asked, "What's your major? Something other than French?"

"Yeah, I'm in biomed," Cecile said, meaning biomedical engineering, which Max understood as a nondescript but difficult STEM major netting an enormous salary upon degree completion. "I like it," she went on, almost murmuring. "It keeps me busy, but it's a kind of work I don't have to think about."

"I'd like to do French, too..." she added thoughtfully.

"Your French is good," Max said, glancing to meet her eyes.

They went on like this for some time, coasting on a pleasantly blank, featureless surface, collecting basic facts, like that they were both 19.

"19," Cecile said.

Max was contemplating her empty cup, which was hanging from her little finger, in front of her knee, close to his right hand, which was stroking the duvet.

"Do you have a fake ID?" he asked.

Cecile shook her head. Her brow was furrowed. "I don't usually buy alcohol. The wine was a gift from Edward."

Max gave a shy, pleading look, which Cecile correctly interpreted as a request to explain "Edward."

Speaking for a long time, uninterrupted, she illustrated her long and complicated relationship with Edward, a business major ("a total psychopath") who sold, among other drugs, cocaine—Cecile's favorite, she admitted. At the start of their relationship Edward had supplied her with endless free product, then without warning had begun to charge her. In December, she asked her dad five times to replenish her allowance; by then Edward had shifted into an erratic mode of correspondence, sometimes showing up at her place without notice and with drugs and cash in his pocket, belt already undone, pulling her down to the carpet right there, almost in the doorway—she said she'd had to cut herself off, to stop answering his texts and calls and attempt (or at least contemplate) sobriety. She specified, truthfully, that Edward had brought the Malbec three days earlier, at which point he had berated her for twenty minutes while pacing in her kitchen and stormed out without touching her. She hadn't seen him since then.

She spoke of all this in the past tense, but her tone suggested that things with Edward were not completely resolved. Max ignored this; everything was irrelevant. As Cecile had spoken they had gradually nestled closer together; their limbs were intertwined. His wrist levitated above the ridge of her clavicle, his fingers bloomed downward and found her neck. He asked, "Can I kiss you?" She enthusiastically said "Yes."

♦

For a while they didn't text; Max imagined it was because they were both momentarily sexually satisfied, and because there was no need to proceed in any particular way.

One afternoon he ran into Cecile on the steps outside [–] Hall. Her skin was pale, almost gray. The sky was overcast and cold; they sat and talked. Her fingers stroked the dark purple scarf she was wearing; her gaze was fixed on a withered shrub at the edge of the parking lot. As they spoke, Max glanced repeatedly at her face until their eyes met.

Max felt the emptiness of his head; he wanted to read Cecile's mind. He had nothing to give anyone, he thought, not even dialogue. If it were February 2020, the burgeoning media coverage of COVID-19 would have provided everyone with an obvious topic for discussion, a shared experience—but it was February 2018, Trump's term was at its midpoint, the university seemed locked in the sort of apolitical trance typical to any neoliberal administration of Max's lifetime. To his mind, the Trump presidency's most prominent feature was its nakedness: the enormity of white American society, the enormity of HGTV and the Cheesecake Factory—the stupidity of the mainstream was exposed. It was unspeakable, but unspeakably shallow and common; it was obvious. There was nothing to say; they fell into a definite silence.

◆

Max had a friend named Hannah who was a stripper and sold weed. One night she texted that she had a bag of cocaine, there had been a party at her place but there was a fair amount left, a generous mound, enough to share with 3-4 people. Max texted Cecile and asked if she would want to meet up and do cocaine with Hannah and her coworkers. Cecile didn't give a straightforward answer: first, she had questions about the time and place, then she questioned the ethics of doing someone else's cocaine without paying or matching; she considering texting Edward, she wanted to see if he could hook her up with at least a dime bag, that way she would have something to contribute. "I'll let you know what he says," she said. Max waited until it occurred to him that Cecile would not update him, that the whole conversation had been a smokescreen, and maybe there was no way forward for them...

As he was falling asleep, he received a video message from Cecile. It was a video of her getting fucked in the shower; wet strands of brown hair were plastered across her face; the caption read "revenge feels so good" and was marked with a "dripping" emoji, meaning her pussy was wet, not just from the shower but from having her brains fucked out. Max guessed that the message had been sent to him by accident; he hadn't done anything to merit revenge, that wasn't even arguable. Cecile soon texted that the video had been intended for someone else. Max saw that no response was required—and that he was a fool!

◆

Cecile was not the only brunette in our French class. There was at least one other: she sat in the back row and was perpetually hitting her Juul; she exuded an energy of lethal anger and seemed romantically involved with Georges, a French exchange student who made no apparent attempt to speak English—he was cute, tall, well-groomed—somehow being "all French," the "thing itself" as it were, made him seem to Max a total cipher. Then there was a girl with a dyed red pixie cut and peach skin, ostensibly the type to enjoy dancing with light-up hula hoops at music festivals; Max found girls of this type intriguing but inscrutable and unapproachable. He made a single pass at her (he never learned her name but only thought of her as "rave girl"); it occurred one week when the groups were shuffled. Our instructor, Thea, a grad student, noticed Max's ponderous silence during group discussion. She asked what was inhibiting him.

"Je pense que..." Max trailed off. "Je pense… quelque chose… mais… je ne sais pas... comment tu dis en francais."

"Qu'est-ce que c'est?" Thea asked, blinking, with an expression of mild impatience.

Max hesitated. "Je ne sais pas… I want to go to raves… I want to be someone who goes to raves, but I don't know anything about them… does anyone?"

The rave girl looked at him. "I go to raves."

Thea cut in: "D'accord, maintenant—*discuter*."

◆

Really the end of things with Cecile had occurred only as a reflection; it occurred as Max was undergoing a series of changes. First came a ghostly phase of reading; at first he read novels, mainly Russian and French; then he turned to the collection of art books at [–] Library; after reading books on Michelangelo, Auguste Rodin, and Egon Schiele, he was ready to drop literature and writing; he considered taking up painting or sculpture. He watched at least one movie every night; sometimes he watched two.

He began to imagine a movie that opened with an image of the morning sky. The sun rose over a natural landscape with houses, telephone poles, birdsong; it was as if he'd seen it before but couldn't remember where. Some nights he would rack his brain and rewatch the first minute of every movie he could remember, searching for the haunting image, which he thought of as "the real thing," but never found it—which partly explains why he watched so many French films. Some French directors seemingly knew that their films weren't approaching "the real thing"; instead of aiming for reality, a director like Louis Malle, for instance, would opt to make a film like *Le souffle au coeur:* benignly erotic, with characters doing mundane tasks like dressing, eating, brushing their teeth, but always in a state of erotic agitation; films of mundane but distracting activity. Malle and other French directors made distracting films, films intended to divert the viewer from the lack of the real thing.

One such "distraction film"—and a particularly decadent example—was Maurice Pialat's *A nos amours*; even its title apparently meant nothing.

It depicted the coming-of-age of a beautiful 16 year old girl, a favorite subject of French cinema. Max sensed from the start that the film existed mainly so that Pialat could get paid to gaze through a camera lens at Sandrine Bonnaire, also 16 in reality at the time. In one scene, her character sits up in bed to reveal to her mother that she's started sleeping in the nude; the camera eye seems to tunnel into the smooth white plane of her bare back. As it cut to the next scene, Max's laptop started buffering.

He was sitting in bed, gazing at the screen, still seeing Bonnaire's figure in the afterglow, projecting over a frame that was dark, indistinct, architectural; gradually both images faded and were replaced by a non-image, a total nothing. Max asked himself if he was dreaming and decided, no, it made sense; it seemed obvious that the cinematic image concealed this inner void. What surprised him was that the nothing seemed to deepen; to echo with impressions of motion; it seemed muddled by Max's consciousness, his thingness; at some point he started seeing dollar signs. He heard the ringing of coins and the crisp bellowing of dollar bills; his only thought was "$100,000,000,000,000,000,000,000,000,0

00,000,000,000,000,000,000,000,000,000,000,0
00,000,000,000,000,000,000,000,000,000,000,0
00,000,000,000,000,000,000,000,000,000,000,0
00,000..."

This vision had a powerful effect on him; it left such a mark that he met with his academic advisor the next day to discuss transitioning to the college of business and economics. He had lost all interest in being any kind of artist.

♦

Max's fatal flaw may have been that he could only concentrate on the ineffable. His essay on *King Lear*, which he had written after leaving Cecile's apartment on the morning it was due, had been graded B-, but it could have earned an A if he hadn't determined to focus on Shakespeare's "metaphysics." His thesis was that Cornelia's rebuke of Lear, her "nothing, my lord," is reflected when Lear is stuck outside in the storm—because the storm is "the nothing," haunting Lear as a specter of meaninglessness. "Nothing" and "meaninglessness" were interchangeable. In a parallel reality, he might have added some musings on the "metaphysical architecture" of the Globe Theater, but it would likely be affected by the same compulsion to write about "the nothing," so gradually, his approach would degrade to the level of crushing the topic repeatedly with a rock; he would return to a default state of nihilistic idiocy, he would turn his attention back to the void.

While drinking Cecile's pussy he had focused on the pulsing of his tongue, the rhythm of suction, the tension in his jaw—but these intricacies were developed in service of something he imagined to be impenetrable and indestructible, Cecile's orgasm; in his mind, he was doing nothing, avoiding doing anything, skimming the surface of an absence. The same principle applied to fucking in the missionary position: to achieve Cecile's orgasm, to coax her orgasm out of the mystery of their sex, required on his part a sustained act of self-deception; he closed his eyes and imagine himself as nothing, nothing but an automatic and forceful motion; he opened his eyes and saw his cock sliding into her pussy and his mouth fell open in awe, then he felt a premonition of sorrow.

♦

He hadn't had much success making friends, especially within the English major, which seemed increasingly like an infirmary for fans of Harry Potter, less so a program for people who shared a passion for books or writing, or a shared belief in the power of language. Thus it didn't mean much of a social upset when he defected from all open mics, etc., and started to attend business club meetings.

For the first time since high school, Max found himself interacting with "normal guys"; more specifically, guys who wore Vineyard Vines t-shirts and Timberlands, got blotto every weekend, organized in alpha-beta-delta hierarchies, and played Rocket League covertly in crowded auditoriums. In meetings, they were always on their phones, passively listening or sounding off in conversations about the stock market. Their collective favorite porn star was Lana Rhoades, who even Max could appreciate was evolving to look more like Bella Hadid. He formed a pact with a freshman named Tyler—a similarly meek, introverted finance major—to become workout partners. They were both surprised by how much they enjoyed lifting weights; it was easy, automatically rewarding, yet they were slightly surprised to agree that it was not the answer to all their woes.

Max had entered a scene of young men who would tolerate anyone on the basis of "networking," a practice geared toward asserting dominance over as many people as possible, easier when more people work in the same field and have the same goals. His phone flooded with new contacts; for the first time, he gained access to parties in the frat houses on the hilltop on [–] Street. He took rails of cocaine in an LED-lit bedroom with Edward, Cecile's ex-boyfriend; he discovered that Edward was 6'3", pale and thin, always impeccably dressed, with an energy of anger and violence.

He found himself in spaces where sexuality was really liberated, where you could walk the floor with a bottle of vodka and pour it down the throat of a tiny blonde in a romper; it would splash on her chin and trickle down to her chest, she would then press her tongue to the tongue of her friend, a young Asian woman, their tits would press together and their glazed eyes would flutter closed, they'd both look at you and smile with white teeth like Notre Dame collapsing in flames; yet he saw nothing in this, it wasn't even a spectacle, even his orgasms were zeros, alcohol was water, the bottles lined above the counters in the night-clubs were zeros. Suddenly he phased out of the world of parties; he invested all his free time preparing to enter his new major, "Business," a word whose meaning remained obscure.

◆

At the start of the Fall semester, Max noticed that his life was approaching a state of perfect order. He had an internship, he took walks along the [–] River, there were Adderall-fueled study sessions, porn binges, club meetings on Tuesdays, occasional nights out; it was all becoming fixed, everything fit and flowed together, yet it was a life lived at the periphery of an object that remained impenetrable. Max had installed himself in a new life that was markedly more pleasant than his old one, yet it was totally meaningless. Such was his contentment, it took him a while to notice that the university had deposited a refund into his checking account; a few writing scholarships had brought it above $3,000. Max didn't check the exact number, but seeing more than three digits in his account brought about a period of reflection.

Once again, everything changed; this time, he consulted no one. He applied for a passport; at the same time, he stopped attending classes. While waiting for the passport to process, checking off items from to-do lists, he spent whole nights on lounge chairs in the library, sometimes reading, mostly scrolling social media and listening to Pink Floyd in headphones, revisiting their complete discography. He found a strong feeling of exploration in their early work; they seemed to get lost in a wilderness of sound, then gradually extract and refine elements from that wilderness. In this context, their later famous albums seemed greatly refined.

As the weeks passed, Max returned to *The Dark Side of the Moon*, the peak of this period of refinement, which had been his introduction to Pink Floyd; the first time he'd heard it was the first time he took acid. For what seemed like hours, he had poured himself through playlists, vibing and imagining what would come next, following the sequence of notes; it all seemed completely new. Then Max could sense something in the foggy distance of consciousness; then it occurred to him that there had been a band called "Pink Floyd," that they had an album called The

Dark Side of the Moon, a sleek and cosmic title; its album artwork was a ray of light on a black background, entering a black triangle, passing through the other side, becoming a rainbow. He could see a room where members of Pink Floyd were gathered, intensely focused on a shared creative inquiry, a journey into consciousness; he saw it projected on the void. Listening with closed eyes, the living room had disappeared. In the dark, he saw infinite eyes, and the reality of the room seemed fragile, sheer, and numinous, like stained glass. The hills in the unseen distance, beyond the walls, appeared to be the many heads of a dragon-like god, a demiurge; he saw them as Mount Rushmore heads, sinister. He felt the head's gazes striking through the walls, seeing everything but not seeing him because he was, and always had been, invisible.

♦

Max's passport arrived; in the photo, his eyes were wide and full of apprehension. Most mornings, he'd been waking with a jolt from the same dream: drone camera views, contours of skyscrapers etched in shadow. At one time, he might've journaled to speculate about this dream, but not anymore. It didn't take much scrutiny to view it as a vision of empire: an opaque system of city-sized computers, all gleaming, surveilled by cameras and armored police trucks. Every dream ended in a mansion in stone mountains, water rushing from a fountain in the courtyard; there he made love to three blondes on a white couch. He was in ecstasy, but felt no emotion; the dream had undertones of panic and paranoia. For the nights leading up to his flight he didn't sleep, only meditated.

Some of his more intelligent classmates, aspiring stockbrokers, seemed to adhere to a peculiar code of discretion; they seemed to understand about each other's goals that they were immoral, that somehow they related to matters of the occult, that there was a share of evil in their enterprise, something left unsaid. Tyler, who drove Max to the airport, was increasingly raucous and vulgar in social situations, yet when he drove he was quiet; he listened to trap music with an attitude of subtle attentiveness. At the airport they hugged for the first and last time. Max did not reveal where he was flying. His body was found three nights later, mauled by sharks, wrapped in seaweed, washed ashore on the south coast of Finland.

Lakehouse

The sky was pitch black. An opaque cloud covered the whole sky, but it was invisible. Anna was standing on the deck with eight other people gathered around a varnished tabletop sectioned out of a tree trunk. An LED lantern threw blue-white light on everyone's face, but most of the faces were turned so that their eyes did not gleam. Anna's face was lifted, peering with difficulty at the edge of the deck, beyond which torrents of cold wind rushed in sonic confusion, faintly audible, drowned under clamoring voices and laughter; the conversation had fallen in on itself. On Anna's left, unseen, three boys were exchanging names of obscure bands, a ritual she had always found vulgar and vain. It oppressed her, but then everything seemed oppressive to her. She knew she was depressed and sincerely wanted to change. "If I don't assert my existence," she thought, "then I will disappear." She would have to make for herself a reason to be there—but ardently as she pondered she could not imagine what that reason might be.

"I'm going down by the lake," she said, apropos of nothing, minutes after her mind had fallen silent. The sentence came to her and she spoke it instantly, just to hear her voice. As she said it, Anna vaguely thought she was talking to someone, but she had not started a conversation with anyone, and no one responded; her words dissolved in the ambient static of voices. "I'm going down by the lake," she said again, this time feeling profound. She could almost see in the black shade of the rafters the massive waves of the lake sharply rippling, magnetically ebbing in resonance with her own thoughts, most of which were inexpressible. A hand touched her shoulder; she turned and saw the face of Audrey, her only friend, whose parents owned the lakehouse. "You're going down there?" Audrey asked, holding Anna's gaze with surprising intensity. "Do you need a raincoat?"

Anna was mesmerized, not only by Audrey's dark brown eyes, frequently described with the cliche adjective "mesmerizing," but by the total effect of Audrey's personage; her skin shone as if enchanted; her grayscale deconstructed knit dress was obviously Rick Owens, which Anna happened to know because Audrey had tagged @rickowensonline in a selfie she'd posted to Instagram a few hours ago, but it was also charged with the dark enchantment of high fashion. "Do you need a raincoat?" Anna could not parse the meaning of this unexpected question. Apprehending her friend's vexation, Audrey clarified, "There was a sale at Nordstrom—my mom bought like five raincoats. Come on, I'll show you."

She took Anna's hand and led her through a sliding glass door to the house's spacious main room, where thirty or forty people were dancing in the negative glow of three enormous Palladian windows. They tunneled through the crowd, seeing in strobe light flashes silver bracelets and necklaces, ouroboros earrings, tight black t-shirts and dresses, exposed biceps. They went up a staircase, past exposed wood beams that bisected the lofty gloom of the vaulted ceiling. The central beam supported a broken chandelier, unlit, that no one noticed; looking down from the balcony Anna saw that the strobe light was attached to the top of a giant speaker blaring electronic music, blurring digital tones that muffled as Audrey closed her bedroom door.

They ducked through the dark bedroom into a bright walk-in closet full of clothes. Anna's first thought was that she could comfortably live there, that it was big enough to be a servant's bedroom. "Sorry for the mess," Audrey said, inaccurately, as a proprietary gesture of insecurity; the closet was in perfect order. She started sifting through one of the racks. Anna read the labels on the clothes—Prada, Gaultier, Marni, Balenciaga—with a pain combining dread and hunger that made her dizzy; Audrey's neck-length hair and diamond earrings shone in the track lighting; a sudden chaotic motion upset a Bottega Veneta shoulder bag from a shelf. Audrey groaned. "I thought they were here," she pouted, crossing her arms, looking at the bag that fell. "My mom must have taken them. I'll check her room."

She exited soundlessly, giving no sign for Anna to follow. Anna drifted into the bedroom and paused, unsure, by the bed. The white duvet cover was blue in the silk dark. She sat down. "What was I just thinking?" she gasped, glancing at the circular window cut above the bed like a solar eclipse. Shutting her eyes, grimacing, she tried to recall an impression that had passed through her mind, her heart, whatever, a moment ago, something complicated, incomplete, yet deeply felt, but it was lost; its absence rendered the room unintelligible.

◆

Osamu saw black blurred machine-like night sky; metallurgy of gunfire vibrated his abandoned PS5 controller; red blurred the darkened room, glinted glass in the kitchenette, fell on the black fabric of his clothes; he was curled in fetal position on a floor mattress, silent and motionless. Instagram lit up; he scrolled without parsing meaning from the content; it seemed both nondescript and abrasive, possessed by demon faces. He was learning to lucid dream, for one reason: to dream about Audrey. He had practiced every night for two weeks. The first few nights were fruitless; the monolith of his intention precluded any actual process; his dreams were black blurred machine-like night sky. Then, having randomly selected and viewed a self-hypnosis YouTube tutorial, he dove to a broader darkness and found a necklace. The necklace was the key: it locked into the formless heart of every dream. Every night he washed it with his silence. He could feel its weight in his supplicating hands; it was real but stuck in the unreal. It could not be pried away; nothing could be done. So, Osamu shifted out of dreaming and simply thought about Audrey—and suddenly he saw her, clearly visible in moonlight, and she was wearing the necklace. She lay awake in the bed where they once fell asleep embracing. She sat up, moved to the edge of the bed, rose, went to the adjoined bathroom, turned on the light, and brushed her teeth. Osamu, watching as a ghost, saw this motion—Audrey sitting up, standing, walking to the silver/steel-tiled bathroom, turning on the light, brushing her teeth—like a GIF, silent, eternally repeating.

◆

Audrey was unlike most people: he resented no one, envied no one. She was adept at the politics of Instagram, and liked and shared her friends' posts generously, commenting "fire," "goddess," and "beautiful," and she was sincere, but only to a point. Nothing impressed her. In darkness, before birdsong, before the light of morning verified the world, her phone was already vibrating, chiming with texts, questions about her party, Snapchat and Tinder messages she might never read. She felt no pressure to respond to anything, no matter what it was; she would respond to some, no doubt, but others—vague texts from boys, emotionally turbulent DMs from followers—did not phase her but registered as a sort of irrelevant gibberish. Her life was basically peaceful; even before she bought a yoga mat it was peaceful, but now she was constantly aware of the perfect automatic peace into which she'd been born and felt a more focused gratitude—not for her parents, toward whom she felt calmly detached, nor for a "higher power," something she never thought about, but for life itself.

All her focus was given to the present moment, and the anxiety that flared in her chest now and then was an anxiety of imminence, of total embodiment in a sole, eternal moment that was so limited, with only finite possibilities, and ultimately just one—which was fine, as long as she had Klonopin. As long as she was alone she felt neutral; nothing phased her, nothing but the imminence of the moment, and most of the time, even that wasn't worth mentioning. Her phone chiming incessantly, waking her, didn't phase her; sometimes she glanced at the screen; sometimes she simply noted her face smushed against the pillow and went back to sleep.

When the room took on a low luminescence, when some color was cast into the clean beechwood floor, she lifted her shoulders slightly and turned her head to see her reflection in the closet door mirror. She felt déjà vu, blinked it away, leapt out of bed, and went to her desk. There was a seashell dish that held a sage bundle and a lighter. She took the sage and lit it. As the smoke drifted to the ceiling she gazed across the room, out the window. The world appeared as two horizontal sheets, parallel fields, rain cloud and unkempt grass, rolling out to a distant rim of black pines. It was still predawn, the light translucent, the brush scuttled and slanted by the storm, snails hiding under wet stones, fog erasing the lowland hills. The lake was invisible.

◆

Anna emerged from her second-floor apartment, descended the stairs, and walked to Audrey's silver BMW. Audrey saw her in the passenger sideview mirror; she was hitting her Juul when Anna ducked into the car. She said, "Hi, bestie," and began to relay to Anna all the social developments she could distill from the texts she'd received that morning. For Anna, Audrey's calmly energetic tone, dispassionate but attentive to detail, was ASMR, and her friend's beauty and the sudden warm sunlight made her smile.

They drove to an ATM. As Audrey reached out the window to put her debit card in the machine, she received multiple long texts from her mother; evidently she was upset. She said first of all that Audrey was forbidden to throw a party that night; secondly that Audrey had been given too much freedom, that she couldn't do whatever she wanted, not in "the real world," and if she didn't learn that soon, her financial support would have to be cut off.

Audrey narrated the texts, commenting on their implications, to Anna. They seemed melodramatic, random, most of all inconsequential. Her parents were in Milan; nothing could stop her from hosting a party. "I love my parents," she said, "but they don't understand that I'm an influencer." If they did indeed cut her off, which they wouldn't, she would simply take the money she had, around $60,000, and finally go to New York and live on her own. "I don't care if I have nothing," she said, "I'll be happy."

As Audrey spoke, Anna slid into rumination. For the past two years she'd been working two jobs to pay rent but had very little money left to live on; she was struggling, and saving had proved all but impossible. Anna often felt that her bachelor's degree was a joke, that she had not figured things out and never would. And so she harbored an unhingedly bitter resentment—and felt at the same time that Audrey was definitely right; if she were to go to New York and live with nothing, then she still would be okay, and would always be okay, even if she had to suffer she would suffer beautifully, in beautiful sweaters, eating beautiful soup, and in the end she would triumph and the whole thing would make for a great origin story.

After the ATM they drove to Walgreens. Audrey asked Anna to come in and buy alcohol while she refilled her Vyvanse and Klonopin prescriptions. Anna's mind calmed as she stepped out onto the pavement. The sun had disappeared; it was cold. Audrey came around the front of the car and put five twenty-dollar bills in Anna's hand. As their eyes met, Anna felt an overwhelming love for Audrey, and as they turned and started across the parking lot, remorse.

They masked and went through the automatic doors into a flood of fluorescent light. The ceiling was covered with black surveillance orbs. There were two armed security guards, one sauntering near the makeup aisle, the other posted by the iron gate to the liquor section, the front of a long line. Anna went to the end of the line, crossed her arms, looked at the floor, and stood.

◆

Osamu had heard about Audrey's party but had not been invited, and she never responded when he texted about it—yet he was sure that the lack of invite meant only that he was automatically invited, that it was taken for granted that he was and would come.

All day leading up to the party, he was in ecstasy, except for a few pained moments. The first pained moment came in his dream. It had been an altogether chaotic dream, and uncontrollable, which signaled to Osamu an inexplicable drop in his concentration, disheartening in itself. The end of the dream was an image of Audrey, strikingly vivid. She was naked, looking straight at him, and the necklace, which usually hung at her collarbone, had fallen to rest below her navel. Osamu woke immersed in total bodily discomfort. Why had the necklace fallen? Why so low? He tried in vain to analyze the image. Its mere memory sent shocks of pain through his head and neck. It was barred from him; he had no choice but to shrug it away.

He was determined to appear to Audrey as a beacon of pure red sunlight, pure confidence. All the contents of his closet were audited; he thirsted for the perfect outfit; when nothing seemed adequate he was plunged in the throes of infernal fury. He cursed his poverty, his mortality. But returning to the vision that sustained his confidence—not so much an image as a total sensation of Audrey, her perfume, her essence blurring with his, somehow involving the sectional couch in her living room—he could only laugh at his insane involvement in petty, material things. Now that all his clothes were strewn across the floor, just one outfit seemed obvious, even inevitable: a black T-shirt, Calvin Klein underwear, black jeans, black socks, black boots. It was minimal, but with his silver Rolex and 16" Alexander McQueen chain he would look like a god.

Later, sitting in his car, about to start the engine, he checked his mobile banking app and discovered that he'd over drafted his account; he was over $400 in debt. As he pulled onto the road he saw that life was chess and he was losing. He could not ask his parents for help, they'd cut him off after learning he was a drug dealer; his bank had already forgiven him once, he couldn't call again. He thought, of course, that he would figure something out—but the shock of the discovery did not leave him. He drove to the party in a state of agony; at one point, prompted by nothing in particular, he screamed.

◆

Undergoing the threshold of the lakehouse Osamu's face was encrypted in algebraic darkness. Audrey was nowhere to be seen. He searched in the crowd, where many recognized him (not by his face, strangely occluded, but by his clothes) and asked if he had MDMA. He repeatedly said "No." He peered upstairs and across the catwalk; it was too dark to see. Then, remembering his vision, he fought through the crowd and installed himself on the sectional, expecting that if he waited long enough, Audrey would appear, happy to see him.

He waited incorrigibly; time seemed not to pass. The crowd dancing as one before him did not seem to alter in any way but swayed in nauseous stasis. So finally he got up and climbed the stairs to find Audrey talking with two other girls in the half dark. When she saw him, her eyes widened slightly with a new expression that he could not read. He waited awkwardly nearby for the conversation to conclude; Audrey's two interlocutors, seeming to realize that he wanted to speak with her, stepped away.

He did not comprehend any of the dialogue that passed between their mouths. Audrey did not understand why he kept glancing at her neck with a look of agitation. Osamu only understood by the troubled expressions and suddenly strange-seeming tones of their voices that the notion he'd carried all through the day had been a mere fantasy; he understood only this phrase reverberating in his mind, "mere fantasy," and finally saw — when he whispered something in Audrey's ear and pulled away to look at her and she shook her head with a look of awful misconception—that the heart of beauty is cruelty… that *beauty is always cruel…*

Then Osamu, wanting to throw himself down the stairs, simply walked down and out to the porch, where someone offered him a white powder.

They said that they didn't know what it was, probably ketamine. He took it off the blade of a key; then, almost immediately, he thought "Fuck, no, it's meth, fuck, it's meth." He stumbled off the porch, not knowing what he was doing, down to the lake which he could not see. He saw nothing. His mind poured ancient symbols into the sky. He tripped and fell, and his skull hit a rock and cracked like Pandora's jar.

◆

Anna was driving home. She watched her windshield wipers cut through sheets of cold rain that washed down her cracked windshield and blurred over the halo of road appearing within the limits of her high-beam headlights. The recently paved road cut through pine forest that seemed to go on forever.

Normally she would listen to music, but she felt nervous and needed to concentrate on what she was doing. Her instinct was to watch the road for deer, even though these conditions seemed unfit for the movement of animals; she felt destabilized. Her mind—most of it—focused elsewhere, in the past. She was remembering the feeling that had overcome her in Audrey's room, was holding it and trying to unpack its meaning, which was hard, because it was not something that she could express in words.

She thought in half words like music notes appearing on a scratched surface, disappearing with an echo, repeating and resonating in complicated formations that were vaguely logical but amounted to nothing. She thought with lilting fervor and, as the miles went by, a growing sense of exhaustion.

She'd had one beer. She wished to be clinging to a stuffed animal, a buffalo that someone had given her for Christmas last year, that she loved but felt was no longer appropriate to hold. She didn't even know where it was. Then she imagined her car was a giant buffalo with flashlight eyes, galloping, scanning the road. Her thought rose in arcs and fell into long pauses; with each pause, increasingly, she felt a kind of pain that meant that her life was all some big mechanical riddle, a combination lock with some tumblers visible and some hidden. She was trying, her whole life was trying, to open the lock, but she could not do it.

She felt a growing tenderness for herself, and her thoughts changed from planning and theorizing to a sort of soft, mumbled consolation. It was not true consolation but provisional consolation, numbness, something to carry her into the driveway, up the stairs, into her apartment, into the bathroom, where she immediately showered.

She let the water run over her head, smoothed her hair with her hands, and tapped her thumbs against her sternum. Her head was bowed, her eyes tightly closed. As the water rushed lullingly, in her ears the same thoughts that had complicated all night in her silence suddenly harmonized and came to a point, still with an air of consolation, that suddenly found articulation as a question.

Her fingers groped at her neck; she started crying and could not stop, and she was surprised to find herself asking a question that no one could answer. And glancing at the shower curtain, she tried but could not blink away that everything was contained inside a greater absence, that there was an edge where everything met its limit, and that she would for the time being accept life as a faceless unknown.

Asrael, Descent, or Final Moment in Heaven

Asrael was a minor angel who dwelt in one of the many observatory pods of the seventh hotel of heaven, a spacious, round room with a 360° window overlooking rose pink cumuli in a pure color, pure light sky, beyond which extended the wave-shifting tourmaline disc of the firmament. He was known among the angels for sitting on his windowsill reading via tablet, and by the hotel's denizens as a sort of hermetic philosopher.

Dwelling in a creative heaven, a zone of infinite resources, he was free to fly out over the waters and begin to create—but despite his longing he felt unready; his potential, whatever it was, would only be unlocked through fervent reading and study. After all he was immortal, he would have all eternity to prepare his masterpiece.

His room was the frequent site of parties and symposiums. In these gatherings of twenty or so angels, he defaulted to listening, basking in the interplay of ideas. He was content to play the quiet, accommodating host, seeing to others while continually immersed in his own studies.

Asrael often fell in love; now, he was in love with two angels who were roommates, Serzah and Serathiel. They had attended numerous parties as a trinity—but Asrael was unaware Serathiel knew Saint Michael until the Archangel appeared in the portal of his room on the fourth night of the festival. Meeting Asrael for the first time, Michael silently noted the mark of death, barely visible, on the minor angel's forehead.

Michael was a head taller than everyone else, arrayed in the tenth heaven's highest regalia. Asrael immediately loved him and listened intently when he spoke, though the Archangel's words were few; he had the tact of one who knows his own goodness, and he was good on a higher level. At a lull in the discussion he sat with Asrael below the window. Asrael chanced to ask the question he'd held in mind all evening.

"You know the secret name of the Lord," he began. "If you were to whisper it in my ear, I would vow to share it with no one. My only wish is that one day I should make some artwork worthy of God—for he alone is the greatest artist! The syllables of his name are the code that crushes locks and draws new colors from the water." But Michael tacitly refused.

They went on talking, but Michael fell circumspect; his eyes sought the floor, a plane of smooth opalescent quartz, with a pitying expression. As the party ended, Asrael put his hands on Michael's shoulders and stood on tiptoe to kiss him where his neck met his ear. Michael caressed Asrael's face; his touch resounded with a peculiar sadness.

"Be careful not to get lost in reveries," Michael said. "All the angels know you are gifted, but you are too blasé. You don't seem to know you live in heaven."

Asrael bowed. "I do know," he said—but he was fated to forget the Archangel's words.

◆

Dragons swam by as they rolled and smoked cigarettes of the dried buds of the plant the angels call mind. In low doses mind, violet buds on a white reed, produces a sense of perfect hyperclarity, then hypereuphoria, and in high doses augments the angels' power to alter the codes behind reality.

In hypereuphoria the three angels were embracing on the floor, kissing, their faces merging into one. They undressed and copulated as skylight dimmed to starlight and the glass became shade. "We should go to the crypt," Serathiel said. "I want to try something."

Gradually, psychic barriers all but dissolved, they rose out of lotus petals and put on new clothes. "I have markers," Serathiel said, buckling a silver crossbody bag across her back.

The crypt was the obsidian nucleus of the seventh heaven, below and behind the hotel. As they made the passage, a spinning triangle of diamonds, they kissed, and as the violet-black walls bloomed about them Serzah laughed. "I love it here. Everything is more unified."

Asrael had never been to the crypt, a maze of transparent dark. He thought that Serzah was right; in the shadow, everything was one: it was like wearing sunglasses, watching the world in negative, quiet, but crackling with eons of alchemical data. They descended the angel tombs and entered a room with wheels of fortune engraved in violet neon on two walls.

They undressed again; Serathiel reached into her bag and brought out a black marker. "Draw a ring around my waist," Serzah said, "so I can become salt." After Serathiel knelt and made the ring, she handed the marker to Serzah, who turned to Asrael and made algorithmic scribbles across his neck, chest, and arms. Asrael asked Serathiel what kind of mark she wanted. She said, "All I know is that our souls are forever one, and wherever you go, I will find you; I love you," and anointed his hands with kisses.

Again they fell together as one being, only now there was no image. There was a surging, frictive warble, snarling and screeching in almost color, bending into indistinct voices, infringing on other worlds.

◆

Serathiel and Asrael slept as one being at perfect rest, timeless and dreamless, but Serzah retained a seed of selfhood, and the seed dreamed. In the dream, she was carried by a dragon across a dark blue field surrounded by mountains cloaked in clouds. A light flew alongside her. "You are in danger," the light said. "The guardians are coming to kill you. You must leave at once and go alone." She woke next to Asrael in her room, in the bed she shared with Serathiel. Moving automatically, impelled by anxiety of fate, she departed the hotel and fell into the outer darkness.

A few hours later, still predawn, Asrael and Serathiel woke and lay caressing each other's faces. They ignored the guardians, the white owl spirits, for a long time; then they looked up and met the owls' black eyes. "You have been summoned to the altar of the Lord," the owls said. The angels rose and followed willingly, holding hands until they entered the crypt, where they were violently separated.

Asrael was forced down a long hallway and thrust into a black room; the door sealed behind him. He looked to the right. In the blur of the corner there was an ikon, a framed hologram of a crystal machine with a light half hidden, dancing, inside it. He stared so long at the ikon, he almost forgot where he was, then he turned and beheld the altar of God: a stone table, gold candlesticks on either side, and behind, hung over the entry to a closet-like alcove, a shimmering gray fabric that was also a sort of grimy mirror with leather restraints and chains slung like a black web over its ormolu frame. Asrael watched the mirror-cloth as it paled with a light like an ocean of fog, and the voice of God, a searing electric hiss, spoke from the room itself: "Come forth to be consumed by fire."

In the hallway Asrael had expected his heart to plummet in supplicative terror, but it did not; instead he felt confused. He stepped forward uncertainly. "Do you know that I am God?" the voice asked. Asrael shook his head. "No," he said. "I see the accouterments of a god, and I hear some hidden speaker, but I feel no fear." "The insolence of a child," the voice seethed. "'Insolence,'"Asrael echoed. "Do you not take words from books you never read, and feed them to the indifferent maw of some algorithm, daemon?" He lunged forward and upset a candlestick; it fell against the wall and dissolved in shadow. "Enough!" he said. "If you are a god, cease toying with me! or you will see my face in anger."

He was shaking with anxiety, but didn't know what to call it; he had never felt anxiety or anger, only read about them. He waited for a response and heard nothing. But a moment later two things happened: the light of the remaining candle went out, and Asrael felt his throat cut by a knife, searingly; he gasped. But it was a fleeting illusion; there was no knife, no incision. "I say that I am God," the voice said, but it had changed: now it spoke from inside Asrael's head. For a moment he froze, then he fell on the floor and wept bitterly.

For a long time he cradled himself, seeing nothing, crying and crying, trying to ascend to his pure light form—yet he clawed at his throat, the pain was still there, blocking his transformation; all he could be was blue, the color of his room at night. His breath grew deeper; still he could not stop crying. He could not forget the speaker scorning his head, nor the shame of being eyed by a surveillance camera. So he heard, resting in precarious selfhood, a merciful, rational, thought-like whisper: "You have deigned to seek God's secret name. In your next life you will know him by one name only, and his name will be silence."

Serathiel entered the room. God rebuked her in a higher-frequency language, a blind screech only the highest grace of angels could hear. Asrael, studying her face, heard nothing; in the candle flame and pale godlight, he watched Serathiel's face, her sweet, gentle face!—as she phased from panic to breath to tears, and her tears were cried through the river of his soul, a river flowing through the silhouette of a planet destroyed, the pain of a society crushed abruptly in awkward throes of gravity, oxygen burning in a black hole; he saw she was not listening. She was cradling her clavicle, head bowed, silently crying, feeling infinite tenderness for herself, infinite for-giveness. She felt her love like a padlock on her heart, cradled her heart, and pressed her cheek to her shoulder in self-embrace. She forgave herself for having ignored that all this beauty was a dream. It was still beautiful; she felt certain that the sorrow and pleasure she'd dreamt were real—but what was real? What could she ex-change then, and with whom—for who would listen? to verify her sense of the real?—Life seemed to generate meaning by descending into itself, exploring its own rooms, its own uncreated fathoms. Her next life would be beautiful, and there would be bonfires at night, but not like here. On the first night of the festival, she had stood aside with Asrael in pure mind clarity as Serzah paid homage to the black hole. They had looked at each other, silently understood some-thing, and embraced; then their hearts were one ruby heart eclipsed in bleakest heartache, a pain they could not understand. But now she understood: her heart was one blinding light, one diamond apparatus, illuminating a void; there was nothing else, and her lover was a nothing, a mere sign falling through the sheer diamond filigree halls of her soul; he was destroyed as she crushed into a black marble and into the abyss.

Gethsemane

Death sees itself in the darkling blossom of exit from the moment of the body, an eyeball peering into its own black robe—and in the final glimmer of vision extinguishes to a wide, black river, freezing clear water flowing up to a total horizon, an inaudibly singing circle lapsing to a great glass dome pressed by dark blue waters, the waters that break over the earth at night to wash Sophia's mind in the solemnity of the real, to seek her reflection in the nullifying mirror of consciousness. She sits at her vanity frantically doing her hair, scanning the floor, seeking a jewel that fell, not knowing if she wants to attend the party but knowing she will go; already, her presence is inscribed on the phosphorescent black of the night's unwritten slate; her necklace and eyes gleam sharply; she is lost in the violent shadow of the future, waiting for her Uber to arrive. Her window is indigo panes scratched by thin branches with ovate leaves, cast in the caging panic of missing a deadline, intervals of irrational seizure, a debt reinstated—then the blurring wall, moments like sheets of ice shocking into the ocean, evaporating, slanting the room as she approaches the black door to the stairwell. "This is all a smokescreen," she murmurs into her sleeve, vexing herself, not quite tracking her thoughts. The street lamps are diamonds, cutting; she cowers into the car but cannot erase what she has seen: the night's stoicism, its lack of interest in her, eons of text seared on its face; its face is turning away forever, casting her through the iron filigree door, up the stairs, into the room where everyone is turned away from her; everyone she knows is in the backyard, the light in the bathroom is blue, her pupils wide and black, swimming with unknowing why she has come— and suddenly, rinsing her face, glimmering her eyes, she feels the weight of her unknowing, a monkey clinging to her chest, pressing its head to her heart, praying to be soothed; and yet she is alone and does not pray to be soothed, only to know what she must do, to look into forest and see city, to open her face unto human faces and see what the moth sees, patterns. The kitchen is void of light; they in the living room lay back gazing in silence at the black TV screen luminescing with white and blue lights and fireflies, and *everything is lucid,* and in the other world, strings of glass beads silently turn, glinting, casting a shroud in an arc across her face, foreboding, and the light burns. After the cavalcade: black ridges echoing into absolute slate. Death reveals its alcoves in petals of emotional color: red for the gap of screeching reciting the long survival poem of the world, nonsense, a wire sigil, souls with sunken faces gathered in polyphonic sorrow, whispering doubt in robes of fire; dark green leaves, urgently daubed, hymns of mourning where faint sketches languish in weeds; they are drunk on amnesia, will never escape to life—for they want it but never enough. Death itself does not know the difference between birth and death. The painting is unfinished, and already the flowers have withered, the violet buds are debased by their beauty, their inward concentration, and the slate can be observed self-inscribing, collapsed in one moment, but no one is there to observe it: *everyone in the world is asleep:* such is Sophia's conviction as she walks, not home, just away, into the void, where her texts fail to send on 5G, the silence of God feels like anger, the earth and sky are a swarm of slithering demons, the internet laughs in its mirror, entropy, unbearably bleak, the houses shy from the crumbling drop of the hill and the trees are shrouded in black webs, glistening, breathing through poison wrath, not knowing how this happened but knowing it is real. She enters their cathedral, a matted floor of pine needles, massive silence—and in the shadow, sees herself annihilated, sees unspeakable living textures, gray and pulsing, dissolving into spiders, and heaven is a blue-white laser, a destroying angel that will not open its eye. Gravity tentacles her heart; she falls and folds into child's pose; she checks her phone, desperate for a siren, consolation, but there is nothing, no signal: *alone*, she thinks, *I am alone*. And the cup is very bitter. The slate is scented with a balm of tears, the blue petals unhinge in a flood of memory, abstract to parallax emotions, inchoate shapes, a blue she has never imagined, a fever that burns her illusions and leaves her disappointed. And the cup is an endless hour, a sapphire set off-center in obsidian, fine scratches writing in its orbit, pale smoke unraveling, reading the runes. 888: she dwells as naught in blindness; behind the eastern sky, a light flash on nebulizing tunnels where seraphs, good and evil, flock in spirals, a voice emerging as a frenzied line, fire in war, a sword so bright it sings—but she sees none of this. Within and beyond Sophia there is no divide, only night, continuity of matter, no image, no joy, no motion, no seeker; yet she knows and feels that the dark itself is the love of God. Only at rest does one discover their true power. At night, kissing the earth, the eyes open or close without difference: light vanishes; dark is constant. Thus the world negates itself in love to be renewed; dark is its elixir. It is the gentlest kiss, a stillness stronger than joy—what could lift her from it? only this: a portal of pure light, pure color, opening between two trees; its path crosses her body, calling her. She rises out of child's pose to go to the other side, where she finds gravel, a service road; she staggers uphill; the road enters a cemetery. Her feet weave by instinct through stout headstones, obelisks, crosses clothed in mirror-like shadow; she moves slowly, encrypted among cloaked forms, a mirage, an invisible landscape watching itself. Then, summiting the hill, she is captured by the vaulting violet curtain of the sky, a lone cloud absorbing the thousand lights of the riverside town. She sits in the grass and peers across the downward slope of the hill, out to the horizon, the ridging line of the mountains; east of the river, on her left, a red light pales the underside of a smoke plume. Trees sever the shifting cemetery planes from the dark pool of town, where the lights are chaos, blinking, drawing out fragments of world space; light floods the interior gaps of a parking garage, flares as orbs in the mountain shadow, searches the highway; the river is a mirror, clear and calm, skewing lamplight where it dives into the curving shade of a bridge, into the other world. In the mountains' crux, in the distance, the southern sky enters the invisible. The earth, the graves, the Venus star—all invisible, waiting to be called at any moment into light, into matter. And all of it is sad. Sophia's mind is pouring into space, merging into more data than could be sought in one night, and she does not want to return to the visible. But the hand of God grips her heart, bidding her to go, so raising her hand to her teeth, wincing, she nods, *Yes, I will go,* and goes down.

preliminary note on balenciagafication

GOD's voice is not thunder but lightning: thunder is only its shadow. he sent the voice into moses' head as an obliterating sonic blast; none but the prophet could survive hearing it. GOD appeared to israel as a blinding pillar of fire. the law could only be communicated as fire, the same aethereal lightning extracted by tesla in 1899—because this is the substance living <encrypted> at core—*reality is a hurricane*—mass lightning ebbing like water, ultralight filaments screeching as they spin and collide. core is a reactor concealed by rotating metal panels; at intervals the panels lapse and the core is partly exposed, but never exposed to the surface, so no one sees, or one sees only without looking, and never as one alone: only as multitude. the hajis circling the kaaba en masse mirror this oscillation and charge it across worlds, crucially: the hurricane calls for a path of transference, ultralight needs a pathway into the world. tesla's experiments were only the visible proof of a poiesis that had already occurred in classical music, first with the early discovery of *fugue* or *canon* <κανών, latinized as canon, means 'law'>, and apotheosizing throughout the 19th century as composers such as wagner, mahler, dvořák, verdi, and tchaikovsky recalibrated the orchestra as hurricane in material refraction, violin and cello filaments assembled in a vortex striking up towards heaven. that these symphonists came to know and use electricity before its appearance in the realm of science is quite clear; tesla's conduction is in this sense a footnote to a century of gradual divine-electrical emergence. in dvořák's symphony no. 9 canon occurs as a refraction of the law of oscillation <return, rise and fall> in nature: even the gentlest sounds are drawn from a primordial, obliterating lightsound, the same lightsound that rises to assert itself as law, fury, reality and hurricane in the final movement. it recalls YHWH's war of plagues against egypt, an assertion of power sublime yet irrevocably intelligible; exodus' key astonishing element is the intensifying rotation of plague after plague—it escalates as a symphony whose emotional content phases from anxiety to terror to darkness to silence, where one must face their own shadow—the promethean technologies, language, number, seacraft, divination, medicine, all dwell in one dark silence, as do the planets in their orbits... the effect of the first rotation conducts into the second and so on, harmonizing in time. interval is a technology of temporal self-optimization: not optimization of space to create a portal, but optimization of time, sound, signification as processes to *conduct truth from beyond*. interval makes truth, godlight, never visible in space, intelligible in time

<because its abode in the desert {ultraviolet} has been sealed>.

Symb•lSoundscribbll:ng3◎ ⌘

The earth soundscribbles in its trembling, in selfdarkness, in anxiety. To soundscribble is to draw by emanation *as if* automatically, conscious only of a will to draw, a vying for some unformed mystery, something hidden in the very trembling: a double frequency, a white-gold orb floating in an alcove whose only portal is microscopic. Such a portal lapses out of light and is forgotten; disoriented, tranquilized, the earth nuzzles in selfdarkness. The earthsound in its constancy is anxiety's calm surface.... Where the senses alight on silence, when time fastens to the frequency of open seeing, the earth sees Nothing.--It sees itself. The earth selfeffaces voidly, senselessly, its gaze a selfdefeating passion; its only rest is pause, its only sleep to blindly crush, and its dreams shock out from core to orbic ceiling, bluely flaring, scratching, writing; its inconsolable murmur sounds from smoldering runes, quiet prophecies always already verified. Earth without Nature: *a priori* privation, an anticyclone abandoned in throes of ecstasy and wrath. Its ecstasy is incense in dark temple halls, its wrath a gesture of history selfdeleting, falling across black slate; from its vacillation within such shapeshifting extremes it contrives the fire-like process of soundscribbling Nature. Nature is an *aperture*. As Nature's thought pauses its path dissolves asunder; it is immanently capacious, never predetermined. It falls up into drawing as a steel-stone plate colliding over another, ebbing, warbling, striking green saplings with silver fire over rain-wet gray stones*~^^,, vents concussiondread in bliss mud flows, tangles to and fro in time, breaks its own archways by fateful blurred accident, presses leaden boldness unevenly into branches decrying wordless epiphanies, exact thorns, truth without meaning, apotheotic bitterness, selfavalanche, stormreflection图A tree rises in Rilkean awkwardness in parallel storms that never touch; the trunk stumbles up in imperfect overlonging for the boughs, the epiphany of leaves向The storm is Nature's mirror--for Nature storms within itself; it is malcontent. The one necessity of its antigaze is the crashing-together of trees, their devastated assignations as everstrange lovers poised like ladders over dry creekbeds. Thus does Nature contrive

Love: by blind fall into barren decrepitude, by shaking away past and future, by tracing *desertion* in stormshoulders. Nature is an aperture falling up in ecstasy of drawing; it *can* stop to think but usually does not. Its throes burn too dark to be undrawn. We can imagine Nature stopping to think, resting in uncanny stillness, contemplating its work--but in the midst of such volcanic strife, what would it essay to change by such intervention? It is wont eternal to delve into the same seismic rotation. (We happen by the impossibility of landscapes, the fatal muteness of granite, the ruinedness of all framing… as for such a tactily selfcreating expanse all segmentation, all separation is impossible.) Such antilinear perspective forgoes continuity with Nature. Its only continuity is to split apart from itself and jut skyward in duplicitous conjecture; its struggle-in-rest is to fall apart; its rest-in-war to selfcloak in flocks of birds. Its ecstasy falls forth antigazing in time accidentally, unconsciously, with massive fluctuation, as *seasons*. Seasons *leave* Nature's vents as a mass of fire from the death of a star; their path is Nature's one path of order, a branching path that scribbles back in time by *dream*.).|),) The path reaches dendritic into water and feels its way back; it shocks through stonelight by *touch*-: its touch is instant. What the earth has lost will not be found spatially, even by soundscribbling in space: Nature does not search. Birds, supernovae, lovers all dreamsearch. Perfection is glance, never object, and dream is never. Only never does an image appear.

早上好

blue light
Falling-up: voidsound. Words like the touch of frayed remnants of a dream, unintelligible. Falling-up to wavesurface: eyes open: morning. Air: silence. No particles, no waves, no form, a dream so sad you thought it was real. Lockscreen: 11:11. Window sheer with white light: raincloud. Head under covers, eyes closed: diving to omdark|uncreatedness. Thought attempt: total wall. Rain murmurs against the glass. Eyes open: stormcloud. Trees thrash in dismal wind. Falling-up of history: East Palestine. black smoke. Inhale: eyes closed: glimmer: hallucination: lightsongcrystal: eyes open in a glass elevator: total transparency. Eyes closed: opacity. Architecture: red and blue light: cavelight: falling-up of contour through darkness into form. Voicemail: what falls up at the last minute. Violence: no message. Halo: river of silence: codex:

inertia: hallucination. Eyes closed, swaying forth, cradling shoulders. Divine transparency: divine hiddenness. World spirals down for angels to be felt ascending: eyes open: field of stars. The world saw the smoke when it crossed New York. I wish we were at the ocean. Star-shaped thought: sway forth, cradling shoulders. Contour falling-up through thought to glass, concrete: a satellite: something hidden. Sway forth, cradling shoulders, magnified as architecture. Ocean makes oceanlight, sky awaits being disarmed: thrashing wind: falling-up of flowers. Falling across a sky, a city: red and blue light, no clouds. Heaven is a city falling-up out of glass. Form is something painfully incomplete: nontouch. Falling-up of morning out of dusk: say something. Eyes open: tidal wave: say something b4 it's 2l8. Eyes closed: an apartment building in Kyiv. pic? Eyes open: skylight. There is no elevator. There is no form. Hallucination: text. Falling-up of slate: test: closed utterance: reality is invisible. Ukraine is visible only in fragments: painscreech thrashing in a locked heart. This is the world: signifying without significance, self-ambivalent. Vacillation: viral fascination: UFOs: ambiguity, opacity: reaching to escape opacity: migraine: limit. Falling-up out of illusion: vertigo: a revolution that actually razes buildings. Falling-up of glass:

transparency: logical reality. What reaches for the Nothing resists memory: test: clear scratches: skylight. World spirals down for angels to be felt ascending: closed utterance. Falling-up of Christ: torn curtain. One word for the world: omnibus, a star-shaped book. Vertigo: veil of sadness: I can't see the ocean, only its text: test: vortex: ocean-form: cuneiform: migraine: limit: hyperform. Syzygy: blisssurging: hyperform. Quantum computing: boundary dissolution: hyperform. Microscopic action: resonance: oceanform: magnificat(ion). cryptography. Mark affect. Mushroom cloud: falling-up of fire. Falling-up through death: travel. Heaven is a city unfolding, waiting to unfold still, waiting to see. I'm still in bed, anhedonic, scrolling. Falling across a sky, a city: there is no curtain. I miss you. imu. I had a dream so sad I thought it was real. When I woke up it was all gone, no words, only voidsound. The sky was bright with one stormcloud sending rain to attack the window. I pulled the covers over my head and phase shifted with telekinesis. I'm trying to recover something: a window to the sky. Eyes open: trees thrashing in dismal wind. I'm trying to recover something: a camcorder you threw in a fountain. It had a video of you in a gray coat, sitting on the fountain's edge, brushing mist from your hair, your shoulders. You looked away to the fountain, then nuzzled your face between your knees and rocked back and forth, referencing something. You said something I couldn't hear. "What?" I said. Without looking, you grabbed the camcorder from my hands and tossed it into the fountain. I watched it spiral through the air and fall into the water. I asked why you did this. You shrugged and said, "I don't know." I didn't know, either, but I know now.

Say something b4 it's 218.

—

χάρυβδις
Exploring rocky cliffs near the ocean, you look at the ground and walk toward the precipice, the ground is dark, it's dusk... you look out over the ocean and see it surging up, falling over the sky. You see water roaring, thrashing, churning with selfcrushing force, selfcollapsing, making a vortex–and the friction of this vortex generates electricity, shock waves, a symphony falling up as algebra. The ocean sings its oceansorrow: one can't comprehend this symphony of tender rage, like the heart pierced by barbed wire.. you could

come to this vortex at any point in history, maybe it's always fluctuating, magnetized by beings beyond our ken (and far beyond the scant expressions of existentialism). If there is a moment when we can comprehend oceansadness, that moment is communicated as sound, as aura. Your heart is pierced by this waveform emotion that changes the entire being... but this is not a video of a whirpool in the real ocean, it is an etching of ocean hyperform, a mental form, an image of a vortex on infinite loop burning in mind as a *symbol*—but maybe such inquiry is meaningless, an interesting mask to keep us from facing the real cosmos: an unspeakable, unfathomable, but unbearably *intelligible* nightmare: an *anticosmos* to parallel the unspeakable notion in Wittgenstein's silence—something he scratched in a notebook in a bright room—a suspicion of problems "which no philosopher has ever confronted (but perhaps Nietzsche passed by)", : abysmal thought, nonsense. constant war. wounded light crystal to see is to illuminate crying up in ecstasy in deathpoint 4 instant heal

InfinityCross

I can't see the creation of the universe through this veil of tears… I watch the veil's shifting and anticipate a sudden apparition of demon faces, terrible laughter, a sudden violence of words; I stumble forth in massive uncertainty, in thrashing wind and sharp rain. Then I come to the cliff's edge and see the *worldbeginning*—the ocean darkly surging, ebbing, warping, selfcrushing, making a vortex. Its song is magnetic filaments burning, collapsing up over the sky, searing my eyes with clarity. It is half-intelligible, a clarion call, a symphony of tender rage like the heart violated, the heart pierced by thorns; like history selfdeleting, caving to heartbreak and spite, self-shrouding; it fluctuates in time with the changing rings and reads their resonances; it contrives to open a moment, a gate for communication to fall up into possibility—but the vortex contrives without language: its utterance is closed. And dream-abandoned nights yield no understanding, only tender rage.

If something is communicated in the surging it is communicated as soulsound, as aura of the forest after the escalated fire, of angels flaring up in enmity. Such waveform emotion always moves as change—but if change lapses behind the unchanging there can be no ecstasy, no opening; only, if God wills, a code-bearing symbol. Not a video of the real ocean but an etching of ocean vortex hyperform, a mental form of magnet dust in furious motion—or a still image, a protoform. Understand that birth and death are aspects of the 1 and life is 0. Before birth/death (before the 1) there is a cave; before the cave a wilderness, an unseeing, 0. In the emptiness of the protoform (in its invisibility, its mirrored shield) becoming becomes infinity.

I had a strange dream… I was exploring rocky cliffs near the ocean, it was so dark I couldn't see the ocean, but then I came to the cliff's edge and the ocean was surging, making a vortex… then the scene changed and I was reading luminous stone tablets in darkness. I was reading a chapter from the *Odyssey*, where Circe warns Odysseus that his crew will have to sail through a narrow strait inhabited by two creatures: Scylla, a spyder-dragon that lives in a mountain cave high above, and Charybdis, not a creature so much as a gravitational anomaly, a powerful vortex. Scylla is nightmarish, Charybdis is beautiful—

but Circe warns Odysseus to veer closer to Scylla, who will only devour 8 of his men, as Charybdis will devour them all. So, Odysseus's crew sets sail, and everything is exactly so. This was the scene I read from tablets in darkness.

Nietzsche refers to the dead god as a spyder. Scylla resembles a diagram by Lacan, the complex-weaving sky-diagram that annexes and vampyrizes the soul: *Antigone*: annihilation by moment of purity in the nothing. The diagram is asceticism, perfection, the 1; Charybdis, what Blake called the Devourer, is the selfcrushing rotation of the worldbeginning, ocean hyperform, the origin, the 0. Between the 0 and the 1 there can be no symbol.. only infinite fractions, erasures. The everything is the unity of birth and death in ecstatic, hypersensual, final consciousness, total communication—the nothing is open air, lifespace, ether, dispersal, discontinuity, necessity. The nothing is reality's stark form, the form of facticity, contrast, the exact. Life is nothingness, an opening between the 2, birth and death, which arise as sheer evanescent contours of the 1. To be cast into this void, to be suspended between earth and sky—is a condition of essential anxiety, soundscribbling as path of divination. The image of self as finite vessel floating in existential field is an image of listening, the openness of signlessness, the potentiality of formlessness, the calm of deletion.

Human Shield

We have phased beyond the reflected image, the screen, passivity, mirroring, into the age of virtual reality, triangulation, simultaneity, reversibility, immediate exchange. This entails subject-object dissolution, oneness of subject blooming out in open space, black smoke rising in 3-dimensional white sky, total epistemic access to ongoing war, energy transfer, intuition attuned to the oneness of consciousness in the world in its totality, integration of death in life, oneness with the world as final symphony, ecstasy, detritus of flower star, moment of deletion. Perhaps we have lapsed beyond phasing, beyond day and night, into infinite open night.

We are like the adam assembled from nefarious rudiments and made to drink the potion of the image, i.e., of lightcloaking, hallucination in space, cascading, amnesia, distraction. Yet the potion is weak and operates mostly by seduction; the worldcloaking image, effulgent even in vague swaths of rubble, intoxicating even in dimness, glitches like blinking to expose the dark circuitry of the real, an exposure sustainable as dream-lucidity. Such is Marx's quiet gnosticism: his critique proceeds as that of a dreamer pointing out to dream-figures their unreality; his technē is to resist arrest; to dilate and oxygenate the sphere of lucidity by schism, by dynamic reversibility. Our reconstructed subjectivity may be that of a torch, disengaged from epistemology, suddenly igniting in a chasm of wires; a face subtly altered by entropy; or sex prior to differentiation, vacant will in the wake of the deletion of the other.

Baudrillard described the dispersal of individuality into the world as screen, ellipsis, automatic grid, passive immersion in technophilia, dissolution in obscenity—but that world of the automatism of "Empire," of the West as global hegemonic order, has already vanished without a trace. After 2-3 decades of orbital suspension this system, perhaps bored of pondering its own stability, began manifesting irruptions of violence and change from within itself as if wilfully. 9/11 is so unprecedented, so absolute, it can only be self-caused; threads of ongoing war continue to fall up and evanesce in the smoke of its images: history spirals up out of order. Land's horizontality, the final stage of Baudrillard's ellipsis, has also vanished. From one day to the next we have phased into difficulty, spontaneity, instability, glitching, reversibility, sudden rift: the invisible subject's updated modes of attacking, contemplating, revising itself. Our new situation is characterized by virulence and metastasis of war/technology, the ambivalent gaze of media, and a pained intimacy, acknowledged or not, with any event, be it local, global or virtual. Our simultaneity is to view the cascade of atrocities as *simul*, same, one of several affect-interfaces orbiting in the gridlock of our pods' unconscious matrices.

Marx echoes Spinoza: capitalism, production, metabolism all are unconscious processes, signals traversing a basilisk asleep in darkness; capital operates at the level of the biological real, hunger, i.e., nature; it proceeds as unconscious evolution out of nature, into machinery; machinery devours the biological. Capital is value potential, resource potential, world reframed as standing reserve; its excavator attaches to the cutting edge of technology; thus the eye-mirroring screen centered the amygdala, interest, attention, desire, consent as the most precious capitals; in the new phase it will seek to draw new forms of labor from these passivities. Marx's reality-view approximates that of psychoanalysis: both examine behavior as it relates to lies and the unconscious. Ideology is capital's psychic mode, it occupies perception and the unconscious, its instance is the lie. In an image-captured world where consent and fantasy are capital, the primary instrument of the lie is the screen, the lens, the mirror; ideology occupies passive technologies modeled on the Dionysian flow of *perception* to subvert higher Apollonian modes of *cognition*. The screen subverts by consent, which we exchange for fantasy; we acquiesce to the lie as to seduction.

Self-destabilized, ego annihilated: the transition from a dual subject-object metaphysics to a triangular spatial metaphysics entails a dispersal of subjectivity in 3-dimensional space, space explored by an evanescent being-asunder tracing oblique flares, wan reflections of 3 dimensions: invisible spiritual world, visible physical world, hypervisible virtual world. The 2-dimensional horizontality of the screen arose from the will of the 1 to be mirrored by the 2, to have something to touch—but the metaphysics of the 2 only yielded stasis; the will to touch was always fatally predicated on objects' discontinuity and impenetrability. The static subject-object circuit sacrificed knowledge for semblance, exchange for stability, ecstasy for ego-ice. Now the static, linear exchange of the 2 (1-2) has opened to the metastatic, triangular field of the 3, i.e., a field formed by 3 lines of simultaneous exchange (1-2, 2-3, 3-1). Being displaced, untethered from these vertices, dispersed in space, original subjectivity is also lost in space, which is solitude; after ego, after the evaporation of objects, we have only to comport this subjectivity as precious cargo across open night—and yet our lucidity in this contact is assailed on all sides; the paradigm of simultaneous exchange, of 3-dimensional space unfolding, metastasizing to unnamed polyhedrons, falls away into vertigo, overstimulation, a virulence of metaphysical forms. Depression is often only a veneer of formlessness, of transition, the world's hyperform changing hands with our wanton and prudent deliberations: the peak of Empire's final overstimulation passed under smokescreen in vagueness/

In the worldform of 3-simultaneity the infinitesimal vanishes into the absolute; an action begun in America ends in Palestine in the same instant.

"Infinitesimal," infinite-small, expresses the paradox of the will, the simultaneity of its slightness and absolute consequence. The will is the first and final ground of subjectivity. Contact with original subjectivity makes itself known by bliss-surging, light, dark, flowers, stars, death, the feeling of purity, that of the will unilaterally tethered to emotionstar; contact is voided when the emotional reality of will, arising as emotion from the invisible world, breaks against the vast mechanistic ongoings of the visible world: final symphony: human shield/

Contact is established in hyperspace, teleportation into the field of emotion, falling-up out of baptismal sky. Human shield is love, hyperspatial emotive shielding, the protection of another life-form in hyperspace, protection especially from the reversal of love as evil, and from the fearful knowledge of the human form itself as a beautiful, cruel, tender evil, beautiful in its severity: flaming sword: desolation of Eden. Contact locates pure intuition in emotional ether, falling-up of blissful solitude, oneness of subject falling up as smoke into open sky, knowing being non-self as awake, tethered as an atom orbiting in the outskirts of the 1, facing the 0, facing the void-immersive spatial field of existence in its violent clarity. The infinitesimal contacts the world in its totality.

Heidegger observes how an artwork as (e/a)ffective as *Antigone* "sets up a world" around itself, sets itself up as metaphor and hyperform of the world. The highest art is to channel the emotion-sound of the 1, sheer magnetic lightning hurricane sound... to channel divine emotions, perhaps the 7 emotions with which יהוה/الله is said to have made the world: חֶסֶד, kindness; גְּבוּרָה, severity; תִּפְאֶרֶת, beauty; נצח, infinity; הוֹד, splendor; יְסוֹד, foundation; מַלְכוּת, royalty. These shards bare their distance from the hypnotic negativity of passive light immersion in vaporous inauthenticity\ GORE-TEX in (k)ether\ ἠχώ/

Kiara

K is a slight change of light in the morning altering the fate of the world. The final epileptic ekstasis of the screen, the final image, which has never appeared, appears to her as if subliminally: soothed by the magnetic flowering image glitching, star-like, self-overwriting with excess, she shelters in the open sky of the screen. She awakens 18 times across hours with no sound and peers out of her cocoon at a ray of light striking the far wall, flaring and fading.

Her Skyrim avatar is a Nord warrior with facial scars and muscular frame; he is lost amid a complex, tedious quest. She sometimes plays for hours without completing a quest; she can't stop herself from directing her Nord to mindlessly steal, trespass, and commit mass murder. The Nord is level 80, no amount of people can stop him. K imagines him to steal, trespass, and kill in a frenzy of narcissistic bliss, detached from all meaning; she often explores this mindlessness for hours and hours, sprinting from town to town, killing. Often her gaming sessions end in over-stimulation and she reimmerses in her cocoon and masturbates in the shadow. The image falls up as bubbles before the soft blur, manifold re-flections of desire for the final image, an image eternal but unrememberable.

Her thoughts in the soft void have the violent clarity of speech, but of closed utterance; the in-wardness of her thought echoes as against an in-visible iron wall. The white paint on her wall is chipping, peeling. She is obsessed with an image of a hentai waifu harnessed in a kind of swing, suspended in the air of a blank apartment, getting fucked by a surveillance machine—but she cannot find the image in perfect video form, the form she sees rising in infinite bubbles in a void.

She has noticed how desire decays into disgust, then beyond language, where every identical image is a closed thought with unique metalanguage. She falls asleep crying, watching videos of beheadings, terrorist attacks, and war, and dreams she is drawing the same picture repeatedly, a picture of a girl sitting cross-legged, writing something on her palm.

poems

Falling-up of Darkangel4
See history spiral out of order
in nightfolds of deathcloake
monasteriė lanterne
green veil of incense
assassins waiting on the lake
Theye kant imagine whats beyonde
This will never b said againe
Ø chiral førmæ
Fire in raine

♦

When you hold me my face touches your shoulder
i Love u like oblivion i kiss you with omni-di-
mensional memory
You kiss me like a bright rainbow flower laughing and unfurling
My sadness is burned away and i want nothing
but to go out of this body
and orbit the sun in yr mind a lightfuckcrystal
to trace a circlepath 4 a portal 4 our bodies to
fuck into
i want to see God thru u

♦

I don't raelly know what to write about,
Just look at this flower
this flower I found…
What's it doing?
I can't raelly tell
Its like…
difficॐult to say…
Its petals are burning, flickering, and moveing
glowing with a light that oscillates,
and produces charges like rainbow fire
like a shock wave?

enervating… completeing
like it has somethjpg to say
like it has something to show me
like it has an answer to q question no one knows
I love you little flower
that will devour the world…

◆

Existence;
is to be tethered;
is to be crushed;
by gravity;
om all sides;
U hit your head;
You go undersky;
in the mezzanine;
of God;
dream a path;
thru terrazzo;
Tathāgata;
fabric of pain;
locked circuitry;
U face reality;
Om;

◆

bloodfaceprint appear perfect
walking in summer
with a bloodhand (fall in summer
printed on my nonface i turn
into the other (falling leaf
a falling leaf turns
into the silence of the other
to observe from a distance (desert field
ankles veering (angel destroy

♦

i guess i'll never think again
or only think in star
the thought extinguishes the star
absent the star the word dulls
the world speaks in graffiti
fashion is invisible
i want 200 people in ebbing dance
in an open space at the museum
want space to open into motion
want space to veer like love
this institution will be broken
this flower will open
innocence transform/

♦

energy beyond act
burning obliquely like falconwing
the act enacts itself
blithe untether'd weaponsong
angels tend their sleeping creation
placing lights at the hands~

♦

like antigone or asuka anorexic in infinite field
i want to fuck in sand under sorrow sky
and crash an airplane into the world trade center
for angels love and hate are onesword
to quell thee burningsong of locusts
a separate pain a kinetic cry
a swordsong of silence
in a tunnel thru the sky
they chose me to die

♦

i lost my aura
i gave u my heart
i jumped out the window
u cut the cable

i tucked my head
my shoulders were cut
psalm of falling glass

◆

my saturnine self
forked sideways
on a picnic bench
outside the library
pining to sanctify sorrow
before it disappears
vying to ektouch
iridium foil (see 9
all time all at once
like a forest rotting
a locked throat
being moored to
being unmoored
with vague ideas
with darting eyes
O exposure (sept 4
simul head vapor
floating hills
like latticework like
water separating
i feel like a voodoo doll

like i've been living in
someone else's dream

♦

god
im desperate to be loved
im desperate for someone to love
i came up for air
and knew id made no progress
i woke from the dream
and staggered thru the city
trying to make something happen
but with no potential energy
no practical knowledge
i woke from the dream but only halfway
the sages were burning my laurels
the courthouse was crossing out my name
the devil was laughing
the door was closing
the sages were going underground
and the only light i saw was indifference

♦

destruction of the soul
cut off from creationlight

light almost annihilating the grass
annihilationlight channeled
thru mercy of infinite God
channeled thru distance of image
ruination in the backstage of the image
seen by one alone does not survive
but imprints on the face of the soul
the soul it is destroying
in a nonlinear process
weaving its way back from omega
casting ending on the eyes
a mark the eyes unsee
except in the invisible in prayer
the soul falls up out of perdition
with clear sight of good and evil
for to see is to know to strike forever
to see fine print to know deception
and seeing itself is invisible
a sense for which nothing is invisible
a mind like a sword impassable
a symphony with wings like fire
destiny altered by contemplation

◆

im baptized by morning my face is altered
on the sidewalk with no purpose no mental image

reduced by cold to blind cloth blind bone
reduced by cold to blind featureless unknown
how ecstasy is blindness of hyperextension
how religion is a substitute for patience in heartache
im baptized by knowledge of absence of surface
how earth changes density dreaming faces in
stone
how the dirt rises as text into the screen of the
sky
i will bury my life in the faintest suggestion
baptized in panic of unintelligible murmur
the intelligible charges again the surface the wind
exposes and freezes the skin of my hand
nothing except in symbols exists conducting
sound
but a symbol has no meaning for a symbol
its head dissolves as smoke into other bookstores
its coat is a gesture coveting absent eyes
its voice eyes landscape vanish through black
wall
it is baptized by a meaning posthumous & minor
& the landscape doubly animated of a green-
shroud

♦

i woke up at 8 & stayed in bed till noon
everything is light & dark with dust & i am weak-
ness
most times time is numb & there's no future
what's past was a punch in the face it carried you
over
the past which is a factory of shadows rusted over
some water at the bottom of the bucket makes a
mirror
light reaches into the cave's secret water
to beckon new creatures to be born
i don't remember how it feels to be the ghost of
a window
i don't know what it means to feel haunted by
images of crowds
something severe looms over the bleachers
something unseen in the furnace of childhood
plastic dark hallways where anything is possible
the world cannot be imagined & is not merely a
monstre
the world is one wall floating above the fissure
of time
love is clay dried & drifted by a bitter & prankish
god
a faraway figure whose only want is infinite sand
a room where music doesn't sound like music
a sweet kiss that stings forever & forgets you

◆

everything is burning|everything flickering
the three dimensional world|faintly visible|burn-
ing
stronger in the night|stronger in the night of ab-
sence
the three dimensional world|the unwritten chap-
ter
unwritten in unhappening|preparing for some-
thing
to happen|to be tested by a flicker|the
unwritten chapter
to move within the heart|when everything is mo-
tionless
to work by heartlight|without despair|in labyrinth
simulnight
reliant not on sun or moon|for there will be no
sun or moon
in the moment of truth|only music|no sun or
moon
there will be no need of sun or moon and no difference
stronger in the night|returning in its very leaving

◆

love belongs to heaven
ann demeulemeester spring 2061
healing light
love dwells protected by 0
rotating shadow with still candle flame
my first face cries from a shuddering heart
birth is like a migraine
the body is the mode of tension
the 2 arise from the 1 to fall away at once
the 0 is stable deleting in an instant
all ruination
not in a million years
love belongs to heaven alone
it doesn't belong to you or anyone
and you don't know
you really shouldn't pretend to know
i live alone i go to die alone
not asking to be reborn|not in a million years
a grass with a long stem trembling in the sky
a light with six wings
almost speaking|with no question
the heart is the mode of being carried
the heart is the mode of being carried back

meditations

earth, the planet where i live, used to seem solid and still. earth, the element, seemed identified with stillness, and i counted this stillness as one of four spiritual powers of the body of this planet. then, hiking in the sandia mountains, i watched a mountainside disappear under its own rising shadow. the lower the darkness reached down the faces of the gray stones, the more vividly the stones waved. in the reddening light of the sun the stones and dirt waved too. one wave was water, the other was earthquake and entropy. new mexico taught me that earth is not a stable element, it is only an element of opaque fabric. you can't see it up close: you try to look, it eludes you. when you come to a high point on a ridge and look to the west and down on albuquerque... it's very strange. the sun goes down and your body disappears into the dark body of the mountain. when the light disappears, so does the earth, so does the mountain: there are no mountains, there is only earth, a fabric that reflects the dark or the sunlight. you see this dark fabric as a frame: within the frame is the lighted city: the city looks like outer space. you reflect that you'd seen yourself as someone coming from the city

into the mountains. you had in some sense identified yourself with the city. how strange this impression then seemed to me, an earthly animal,
shapeless in the night, seeing the distant streetlights of an alien city. i looked at the city not
knowing what it meant, feeling at peace in the
natural dark.

◆

the sky is primary: a nothingness where light pro-
liferates and color washes over color; the earth is
painted brusquely on the sky; the river pours up
out of the heart of eternity, ecstatic and clear. the
hills are gods: colossal animals, great half-beings
bowing to the continuity of the river, clinging to
the calm love of an unknown heartbeat, extending their paws to receive life. the hills are mysti-
fied by the river: they long to ask where the river
flows from: the hills have lost their tongues. they
open their mouths, their caves, to breathe animals
into the world: the animals dream: the hills read
the dreams, searching for clues: the humans
dream and speak and write and the hills read their
language for clues. language is a problem: we are
like gods: we have forgotten our true tongues. the
hills are sleeping, restful in their unknowing love

for the river. we, too, are sleeping, but we are not at rest; we are tumbling in the sky, static, fixed between opposite destinies. sometimes one must go to the river: the heart needs to make contact with its mother, to remember where it flows from. the river gives answers only the heart can hear. the river is invisible: only the heart can track its motion. where the earthly lights touch the water, the water reflects their souls. i don't know why i was brought into the world, or if there was a reason. i don't know if i have a soul. but i have seen the souls of streetlights reflected in a river.

◆

i'm going back—before the hills and ohio appeared from behind the trees that tower over dead man's road, before the ice broke and i fell into the creek's freezing water and my dad rushed to save me, before the perfect peace and safety of the bright green grass of my grandparents' yard in the wooded hills—forgoing memory, the firmament of memory, going beyond... i don't know where i'm going, but i know i've been there before, i'm there now—it is something i carry within me, it is something carrying the atom, the electron that is me, the cipher that is called luis neer... it is hard to focus in this hidden place, this non-place. my body is a soft machine haunted by sorrow. i am trying to let go of this sorrow, but it will not let go of me. i am feeling my heartbeat, wearing an old hunting coat to keep warm in the cold night of the desert.

◆

earth: rubble. pewter. bulldozers groaning pulling down walls smearing dust on the air. gray sky and river. obsidian. distant stormclouds. what matters is stillness. still distant clouds. shaking hands. carpet. resting. inertia. being pulled toward a massive enormous heavy thing. emptiness. openness. coolness. daytime. nighttime. sidewalks. air: birds. birds flying, soaring in no space, no time. there are no lines. lines are abstractions, distortions, fabrications. bliss. blur. inside my head is outside. shimmering. nothing shimmering. open mouth. light. light may be waves not particles. which makes sense. light doesn't settle as dust. light is not confusing. i don't know what lights light. air is neither light nor dark. air is invisible. air has no syntax. air is chaos and oblivion. speed. falling. lilting. leaf

♦

cacti are strange... they are the octopi of the desert. when i look at a cactus it seems to return my gaze... and seems to hallucinate me, seems to gaze on some strange beast, some indecipherable linguistic character that might as well be me. maybe the cactus sees a creature covered in spines, eyes made of fire, a mouth of white teeth... maybe it regards the human as an object of mystery and terror. not that i fear cacti: i don't, and its spines don't intimidate me. looking at a cactus… the essential sense is suspicion. a feeling that it is a sentient thing... that it is a person wearing a disguise. even its spines seem illusory; in the event someone touches its flesh, provisional "real" spines are deployed, supporting the illusion—they seem to appear slowly, magically. it has never totally fooled me. cactus may be an avatar for a general strangeness in nature, a creature cursed (like humans) with a codified skin, a forcefield of data that cannot be exchanged outside the body of its own antagonisms. humans and cacti both bare a peculiar and visible strangeness that reflects a general, invisible strangeness that circumscribes our reality.

◆

trying to see what i don't remember—eyes closed seeing shadow images passing like smoke—there are vague impressions of grass, my grandparents' blue ford explorer, sound of windshield wipers—feeling, feeling of dearness, feeling of loss, fearing loss—soft sound, sound meaning rain, silent rain—mostly i remember darkness—what is dark—dark and soft swiping and scuffling, sound meaning silence, silence something that lives outside—questioning, waiting for light, waiting for faces, a birthday party— i don't remember it, but it happened: it was in the yard of my parents' house, a few blocks from the ohio river. the yard was split by a long concrete walkway. tables and chairs. i was under the sky, looking up at my mom and other grown people. they were shadowy, towering bodies emanating weariness and knowledge. my mom put her hand on the back of my head. i can almost feel that. i can almost trace my way to a feeling that isn't there.

◆

'there' is nowhere. this is just a fragile stage, a little space constructed for something to look at, a flat plan to traverse, yellow chairs, blurred objects, provisional simulacra. this version of my parents' yard is a field engineered by a memory system in my brain, a field to accommodate an investigation toward something that will not be discovered. when i look at the sky (when memory deploys its "i," its camera) it is somewhere underground. when i look at the ground i know there is nothing beneath it, only darkness, swiping, a nothing—

◆

there is no world: there are people, all of whom are suffering; there are objects, tools, mechanized extensions of people, prostheses whose phantom weight reflects and relieves the weight of our suffering—all weights being bound to the mass of the surface of things. we are animal spirits born in darkness—simultaneously finite bodies and endless flows of water—cold water extending into a matrix of hard matter, a vast machine void of temperature, an electronic and mechanistic system determined to perpetuate itself. there are cacti, juniper trees, porcupines, all suffering, all holding death and anarchy in the hollowness of their breath. they, too, are clinging to the extreme outer limit of earth; earth is a sentient concentration of gravel, an infinite focus, a focus that may release at the right moment; the moment of the end is unknown. nietzsche sensed the passionate nature of the spirit of gravity: the cluster we call earth is held together by its sorrow. when all our sorrow—the emotional gravity of the world—has dissolved. everything will disappear.

♦

syllable, sophia, katerina, omen, psyche, aura, shiva, azazel, valhalla, omen, ocean, moon, ocean, moon, moon, omen, ocean, moon, moon, ocean, moon, omen, omen, omen, moon, omen, chaos, light forever, moon forever nothing mirrors moon light mirror eye mirror eye mirror eye bright blue moon in raging sky dream of sunlight searing the desert sky dream of blue light in the midnight sky sun in dark face yourself in the light in the mirror fire forest light earthlight heart of peace heart of peace in fire death of heart in holy fire dream of death in secret room dream of love constant sense of doom dream of prison you are weak and small you are standing still you are drowning in silence you are a prophet gazing at ocean sky expressionless with no thoughts you are a prophet you are noble you are loved by sophia angel of wisdom omen angel of dream and είσαι το μόνο πράγμα που φοβούνται

♦

the axis of the meaning of the world has migrated from the body to the screen. no longer is identity or experience produced by the reflection of activities back onto the body, the self, so much as the self and experience are produced by a projection terminally outward through screens, into a zone of reality that is immaterial, hyperspatial, luminous and vaporous. the solid world of rooms and people and clothes and lamps has fallen back into the shadow of this bright, glass-encased vapor—and the human face, the locus of personality, has projected itself forward into disembodied light; no longer does it bear any necessary relation to the darkened body that carries it. that theatre of physical presence, "that entire social and psychological theatre, that entire existential psychodrama, has been swept away by the directive,

interactive behavior of a society without actors"
(baudrillard)—

◆

the manhattan cityscape: a world built on a verti-
cal axis. moving across it horizontally, viewing
from above, there is only a vague and distant
sense of the earth crushed beneath this expanse.
the buildings are all pixelated units combining in
a texture, a supercomputer scan of a topography
that doesn't exist, that doesn't resemble the
earth's original surface (which has been oblite-
rated). the city stands in monument to itself despite not knowing itself as a city. new york is the
"empire state"—but while the empire can know
its own name, it cannot attach any meaning to
this signifier. for the individual living within empire, under empire, there is friction between "natural" and "empirical" states of mind, friction between intuition and reason, between one's own
desires and the obligations imposed by a world
that is ostensibly alien, harsher and crueler and
faster and more excellent than what seems innate
in human beings. for the individual, empire can
mean evil—but for the empire itself no meaning
is possible. it senses itself as historical extension

and extension of a natural order, as accident and inevitability. resting, it dreams silently of itself; when passions seize it there are visions of bygone architectures and (quietly fascist) folk cultures. the imperial mind is subject to waves of anxiety, dreadful remorse with no object, wise and serious sorrow. empire has its own secret and volatile astrology, its own dionysian swells.

◆

the mind is fast—it loves speed—but time is slow. time doesn't pass quickly. it wasn't so long ago that i was sixteen, starved of love for the first time, not quite realizing how low down in the shadow i was. suicide then was a pleasant dream, distant, sweet, like morning wood. the problems that shadowed my first depression were lighter, more poetic, pleasantly piercing, cold like snow. if i couldn't sleep it meant i was sick. it didn't mean what it means now: that i've had an unproductive day, that i don't want to sleep before something has been done, that i'm looking for something. then i was not looking for anything. sometimes i felt sad for no reason and cried to my mom. my bedroom was next to the room where my mom and stepdad slept. one wall of my room was a wood frame bolted to a broad chest of drawers, shrouded with a dark bedsheet. members of my extended family worked together to build that house. it was a two-story house. the first night we slept in bunk beds upstairs the room was plywood floors and naked drywall. it was like a hollow lantern hanging in the night sky. the staircase was long and narrow; voices boomed inside it. my mom and stepdad still listened to talk radio. i talked to a girl on the house phone. i dreamed about us kissing but it never happened. one time, on the bus, she kissed me behind my left ear, but it was just a joke. the bus was chaotic and cruel. i wanted to move into the green bush in the yard, the one that blooms bright yellow one day each year. how i loved to press my cheek to the dark green carpet. in summer i loved to roll around the soft, cool floor. i loved the dark of the den, the windows painted with summer light. that was my first meeting with the earth's immense gravity of love. it was my first time noticing that gravity is a lullaby.

◆

the world is one sound, then another. in waiting, rummaging in the traces of the passage of the last world, one is always blindsided by the passage of the next. no microclass has first access to this phoenix: it is always *something else entirely*, something marked only in hindsight, by the fading of the wing—but all feel the precarity of life in its, that is, the world's dream: one sound, one symbol voided by the next.

◆

eschewing desirability, the world's constancy is perhaps not one of principles, but of *syllables* flaring up into words, ideas, things. it is not that the fire speaks, but that speech flares—and this is an obscure deception, pause-giving nonetheless, in *gorgias*, where socrates checks: *if there is fire, must it not have something to burn?* callicles, the uninitiate, answers as expected, *of course*—but heraclitus might have halted: *no*: first the fire burns itself. the fire before the burning.

imminence

death/ no distance/ no fear/ everything ever clashed in wilderness sound/ raw tired walking silence/ notion of music/one life. distance from anxiety: breaching edifice/ resting the soundless inside the deadline/ distance from *I*/ distance from putting-into-words. constant listening newly possible. breaching the edifice of the deadline/ after the deadline/ dark hollow echo: continue/ existence in the moment of creation is nonexistence\

◆

cultivating grace: everything everclashed in wilderness sound/ existence is discontinuity/ space is continuity/ openness/ vulnerable breaching/ positive void/ evolving toward the edge of something: focus: simplification\ delimiting/ organic attributes/ centralizing process in one vessel/ consecration\ direct transference with technological field\ hyperspace/ field of transmission/ infinite yes: continuity/

◆

imminence: infinite no/ nothing left: everything free. everything/ deferred reality:: nightmist: simulation powered by $100,000,000,000,000, 000+/ no sleep/ no food/ no drink/ quantified presence/ existing capital. response: nothing hidden. available balance/ excess presence/ something too complex to be rendered. desire paid capital where nature was null: cursed exchange/ bloodless. screen: convex mouth/ inner surface. going into debt: encrypted presence/ borrowed existence/

◆

distance/ debt: existing barely/ encrypted blank/ fountain/ automatic meaning/ want platinum credit and $800,000/ convex mouth: untouchable/ no matter/ no barrier/ language is the nothing unleashed on the world/ i should be free but im not/ i put minimal power into something unreliable/ something beyond me/ a process automatic in thought but nonexistent/ swept away/ miraculous/ never/ never/ idk////////

◆

mind racing 100000000 miles dying for new life different life stop void no void everything void now here now life everything somewhere warehouses lofts cups tables colors coats eyes arms interlaced white teeth shining a sectional a secret traveling outside inside outside open world all

open secrets open knowledge open eh482e
kghevnhjvnsanwq-an;ld   isafuq8o9;rjc   hslfi-
cusvijxjiuohlhnlknqkb13-w35r754   54   5489-
55434756t7896076654405584972fanohn348fn80
607ygg76t976076979y6tfctddv355r86t87fvugtf
y5f74r4 ffyiciuiuik-gy769900\\

◆

imminence: mirror/ writing on the mirror/ writing the present on the mirror/ vast hallucination/
moving as human in vast cosmic unifying dark-
ness/ consciousness/ free mobility/ intense mental inscription: i should be free but im not. prayer:
zen imminence: light reflected in water/ surface
tension/ cold air/ falling stone: plop. prayer:
BMW Z-3/ feeling of driving a car: swerve: psychic mobility/ no surface/

◆

distance: writing/ like descartes/ by candlelight/
psychic mobility/ swimming in hyperspace/ still
blue dark/ frozen grass/ fog blurred morning/ in-
tellectual blindness/ pleasing vibration/ hyperspatial drifting/ hyperspatial darkness/ scratching
emotion/ secret blue surface/ dark slate codex/

cutting to the core inscribing the core tablet/
opalescent slate enclosed in plasmid darkness/
the critical work/ original inscription: dark hollow echo/ new life/

Online Writings

Luis Neer

Subtle Body Press, LLC
7901 4th St N STE 8671, St. Petersburg, FL, 33702
www.subtlebodypress.com

ABOUT THE AUTHOR

Luis Neer was born in West Virginia in 1998. His debut in poetry, Extinction, released by Sad Spell Press in 2016, was hailed by Ocean Vuong as "a book wrought from the urgency, charm, and ennui of American adolescence—yet executed with a seasoned and hard-earned intuition for what could be gained when a poem is pushed beyond its facile containers, and into the wild parataxis of an inner life rich with fluidity and contradictions." He graduated from West Virginia University with a BA in English in 2020 and dropped out of the University of New Mexico's MFA in Creative Writing program in 2021. In 2024 he contributed cinematography for and appeared in two films, Paradise (dir. Angelicism01) and Monad (dir. Dana Dawud). Online Writings collects his writings from 2020-2024. He lives and works in West Virginia.